BRYCE

ADDISON JAMES

ADDISON JAMES

CONTENTS

CONTENT NOTES

- Self-esteem issues

- Belittling by family members

- Very minor mentions of past lovers for FMC and MMC trying and failing to seduce another woman

- Plus-sized character who is mostly body positive, but sometimes struggles

- Fighting

- 18+ sex scenes

- 18+ language

PREFACE

Bryce takes place three years before Callum, and is about the early days of Bryce and Mae's relationship.

When I first envisioned this series, it was a duology that started with Callum and ended with one follow-up book. However, I knew very early on that the cast of characters were all going to demand their own stories.

Each book can be read as a standalone, and each book has a happily-ever-after for the couple it is about. However, if you want to know about the larger world of the Crae siblings, I hope I do a satisfactory job of exploring it here.

So, this series began with *Callum,* and before we find out what happens next, I invited you to look back with me and find out how the rest of the Crae siblings got to where they are today.

CHAPTER ONE

BRYCE

"**Y**ou've got to be kidding me," I say, looking bleakly at my sister across her desk.

The look she returns is decidedly unimpressed. Good: Two can play at that game. And while all four of us Crae siblings might be able to be grumpy bastards, I've always taken the cake on that score. So I know I can hold out longer than her.

She knows it too. We've only been having these staring contests for a thousand years now. Sometimes I think we were having them in the cradle.

"I've been with the humans all week," I try, but the set of her eyebrows tells me she's not cutting me any slack.

It's true, too, and that's the worst of it. I've spent a week dealing with human politics and that always leaves me drained. Humans really are tiring, but when politicians get it into their mind to try to pass a law that would allow logging on the mountains that help hide our home, someone has to play the environmental lobbyist and go grease the right palms. And that someone is always me.

I want a meal, a full night's sleep, and some time where I have to talk to absolutely no one if I don't want to. I do not want to get on a plane to anywhere, much less to New York.

New York stinks, and the steel and concrete always makes me feel claustrophobic. And, more to the point, it's not home.

"Look," Celia says, tapping the fingers of her left hand on the desk. "I know you're tired, I get it. But she's been doing the border enchantment for us for a hundred and ten years and I can't get ahold of her."

"Send someone else," I say, just barely avoiding snarling at my sister. My queen, who is usually pretty tolerant of our bullshit, but might just snap back if I'm too much of an asshole. "Send Callum." Border enchantments sound more like his business than mine.

She rolls her eyes. "I'm not sending Callum away when our border enchantment is weaker than it's been in a century."

"Chase." He could get there and back in an hour, and I could go the fuck to bed.

She actually grimaces. "Chase and Heath just got back from an assignment for me."

"So did I."

"Chase took a shot to the neck. He's fine, but you do not want to get between those two right now. Trust me."

So she'd considered asking them, at least. And now I'm the only option left to her.

Anyone could get on a plane to New York. Anyone could march into the shop and demand our border enchantment. But the question is, do we want just anyone doing that?

No. Celia wants one of us, and it's going to be me. I'm the best, and I always represent our pack when we need the best. When we need the job done and done right, I'm Celia's go-to. Always have been.

She pushes a paper with an address across the table at me. "Plane tickets have already been purchased," she says, sliding the printed ticket across next.

I glower at it. Economy. With a layover.

"Bethany's been cooking?" she offers when I look up.

It's not the worst consolation prize I've ever gotten.

***

I barely have time to savor my meal before I'm off to my house to re-pack a bag so I can get to the airport on time.

My house looks like someone hasn't been living here for ages. Not that I do too much with it when I am here, truth be told. But the lack of use is showing, and I have to hastily wipe dust off the countertop as I dig through the drawer for a human ID that matches the name Celia used on my plane ticket.

The whole point of our village is to be out of the way of humans, so it's quite a drive to get to the airport, leaving me just enough time to get through the infuriating process of airport security and barely make it to the plane before the doors close.

I swing my bag into the overhead compartment and then go to sit down. It's a middle seat. Of course.

How else did I expect this day to go?

I'm too big to fly economy, never mind in a damn middle seat. And the humans might not know what I am, but something always sets them on edge around me. They always know, deep down, that we're not like them. And now I'm shoved between two of them.

I close my eyes. It's going to be a long flight.

***

After a connection where I barely have time to eat a meal, another middle seat, and helping three old ladies with their overhead bags, I'm left standing in the middle of the busy terminal at JFK.

Humans really are a drain on my patience.

I get a cab outside the airport, not quite having enough energy to handle a subway today. The smells in those places are always nearly overwhelming for the wolf in me, and there are too many humans who might inadvertently touch me. So a cab it is.

I give him the address on Canal Street and settle in for the ride, hoping I can get this over with. That whatever witch has been ducking Celia's calls will be easy to convince to come back to work, and that I can get back on the plane tonight.

Not that I really want to fly again so soon, but if it's my own bed at the end of it and not another hotel, I'm all for it.

I smell the shop before I see it, the scent masking even the garbage and piss smell of New York. Magic, and a particularly strong reek of it. I wrinkle my nose and brace myself for what's up ahead.

CHAPTER TWO

MAE

I have my alarm set loud enough to wake the dead.

It actually doesn't sound too dissimilar to the bell my great-uncle, who claims he's a necromancer, uses in his rituals. And it has only marginally better luck waking me than it does corpses.

After a minute of scrambling, I turn the alarm off, then force myself to roll out of bed. Coffee is already brewing, and I go through the motions of getting dressed while it finishes.

When it's done, I stumble over to it, dumping in one of the vials I keep in a line next to the coffeepot. In lieu of any cream or sugar, this little bottle will do nicely.

I suck it down, still piping hot. Proper witch's brew, there it is. With enough kick to stop a mortal heart.

Even in New York, humans apparently expect shops to keep something approximating regular business hours, so now that I have the shop to look after, I've found all sorts of new uses for enchantments.

Including a teeny-tiny probably-not-that-serious stimulant spell addiction.

I slurp down the rest of my spiked drink and give it time to fully work while I do my makeup for the day.

By the time I make it downstairs to unlock the front door of the shop, I'm fully awake and ready to face the world.

***

It only takes about forty minutes of me checking over the account books for me to give up. "Greta, you're a bitch," I mumble, watching the red ink turn into a blur before my eyes.

Not only has she kept her accounts in an archaic little ledger book, but she foisted them on me without a single job interview first.

What happened to what's mine is mine, huh? Like proper witches? Whoever heard of witches just giving their shit away?

But now I'm stuck with this damn place, and if I look at this stupid ledger for two more minutes, I'm liable to use it for kindling next time I need to start a fire.

I'd hire an accountant, but even I can read the ledger well enough to know that I can't afford it.

In short, Greta left me a pile of shit I didn't even ask for.

The bell over the door chimes, and I don't have to look up to know who it is. Violet always carries with them a distinct mystical signature.

With a witch father and a demon mother, Violet's magic is a complicated web I don't pretend to understand. It has a certain zing to it I've never felt with anyone else.

"One of these days you'll actually have to buy something," I tell them, stashing the ledger away so I don't have to think about it anymore.

"One of these days you'll have to start paying me," Violet shoots back.

"Yeah, good luck with that," I mutter. I can barely afford to pay myself at the rate things are going.

Violet asks most days. And every day I tell them no. But Violet turns up anyway, always re-organizing the crystal collection, despite the fact that it's rarely been disturbed from how they left it the day before.

Violet always has a pattern in mind, it seems, and I've given up trying to understand. Maybe it's just another product of their strange magic.

I turn back around at the counter, surveying the shop to see that Violet is, sure enough, at the crystals. "Love the top," Violet says, focused on their task.

I look down at myself. It's perhaps a bit daring, but probably not anything someone wouldn't expect of a magic shop proprietor in New York. People like the witchy look, even if the humans think it's a character.

And besides, if you have something worth showing off, you might as well.

"Wanna borrow it?"

Violet looks down at their own thin frame. "Know an enchantment to shrink it?" They ask wryly.

I do, actually, but the bustier fits me perfectly right now and there's no way in hell I'd mess with that.

Violet just turns to their daily task of re-arranging my crystals. "You're not, like, cursing the shop with those, are you?" I ask.

"I didn't enchant these."

Not necessarily a no, then. But probably a no.

So I leave Violet to their daily strange task and turn towards the enchantments in the back.

Most everything Greta kept in the front of her shop would pass muster if a human wandered in. They do, sometimes. This is New York and they're everywhere. They wander in to purchase a crystal or a candle or an orb or something they think is a good luck charm. Most of them aren't even enchanted, although Greta had the habit of enchanting the odd one with minor little spells. No harm in bringing the occasional human a little extra luck.

But the real stuff, we keep in the back. Greta is—was—the rare witch who could actually build relationships among other witches, and people came to her from far and wide for enchantments they couldn't or wouldn't do themselves. She was able to convince all kinds to shop with her.

Now they come to me. I wonder if they still will when word gets out that Greta is gone, and it's just me here.

Not that I've made enemies. I'm friendly enough. Certainly friendlier than most witches. But I'm no Greta.

But Greta is gone. Apparently on some semi-permanent beach honeymoon with her secret beau, and she left no forwarding address. Just instructions on how to keep the shop open that look like she wrote them as an afterthought.

Sure, Greta. Just leave your life behind. I'm sure bottomless mimosas and sunny beach reads and sex in the waves forever are worth it.

I may be a little bitter.

I try to push it away. Bitterness won't pay the bills.

***

I'm working on enchanting scrying orbs when the bell over the door chimes again.

I don't stop. It's a difficult, finicky little enchantment that Greta taught me decades ago. Not everyone can do it, so I figure enchanting a host of the things will maybe be a money-maker for the shop.

I keep right on enchanting, humming the tone that goes into the orb as I pour energy into them, assuming the chime is just Violet leaving for the day.

Right up until I hear Violet's yelped, "Hey!" and feel a heavy presence intruding on my back room.

Chapter Three

Bryce

The shop looks like a tourist trap, but smells so strongly of magic that I have to fight not to wrinkle my nose as I walk in.

Not a tourist trap then. Very real. And definitely capable of the kind of magic Celia sent me here for.

The bell above the door chimes as I push my way in, and if I thought the scent was strong from the outside, it practically knocks me over in here.

There's a little slip of a witch standing near some sort of rock display, and I look the dark-haired witch up and down slowly. Young. And not just in the way that most immortals look young. Still a child, really. Probably a few years away from growing into their immortality.

I look around and don't see anyone else, but there's a sound in the back, behind some sort of gaudy beaded curtain. My lip curls. If it weren't for the stench of magic, I'd think this place was a human's, play-acting at witchcraft.

I follow the sound, ignoring the child's yelp as I push through the curtain to the back.

The sound is coming from a pretty witch, humming to herself as she cups her hands over crystal orbs. There we go. This is what I expected, what I thought of when Celia sent me here. Proper magic.

The witch ignores me for a moment, but I know she knows I'm here. I'm six and a half feet tall, for starters. Hard to ignore even before you factor in that prey can always sense when a predator is nearby.

Right, don't say that to the witch. She probably won't take kindly to being called prey. But it's true. The wolf is a predator, and nearly everything else is prey to it.

Her back is shot with tension and her humming stutters for a moment, but she continues on with her task. I don't interrupt. Sometimes the best way to get your query is to wait it out.

Besides, who knows what awful things will happen with the witch's magic if I interrupt mid-spell?

So I watch her as she hums away, taking in the witch Celia sent me after.

Gods, is she short. I'm not even sure she'd fully reach my chest if I stood directly behind her.

She's also dressed… well, put it this way: with my height allowing me to tower over her and the way her shirt is cut, I can see straight down her top. And what a lovely sight it is.

I shake myself. I'm here for work, and I don't fuck around when I work.

She finally stops the creepy humming. "Can I help you?"

"Greta Snow?"

Her shoulders go tense. "No, I—please tell me she doesn't owe you money." Her whole body slumps as she says it, as if just the thought is enough to knock her down.

Is Greta really so irresponsible that random werewolves knock down her door demanding money? Do I want that type of witch laying one of our most important security measures?

"No. Do you know where I can find her?"

"Beats the fuck out of me. You find out, let me know, alright?"

I resist the urge to snap at her. Her flippancy knocks against my exhaustion and frustration, and if I were a less practiced negotiator, I'd say something that would cause permanent damage. What an annoying little witch.

It's long confused the fuck out of everyone why I, grumpy Bryce Crae, am the diplomat of our pack. But this is why. Because I can control myself. Because I don't have to be peppy or even nice to get the job done.

"Greta Snow has business with Celia Crae, queen of the werewolves," I bite out. "And I need her now."

She raises an eyebrow. "As ringing an endorsement as that is, still can't help you. Haven't magically found her in the last ten seconds. Believe me, I would if I could."

"Am I in the wrong shop?" I demand.

"If you mean, is this Greta's shop? Then yes. But I still can't help you. Greta straight up left two months ago."

"Where'd she go?"

"Again, if I knew, I'd... well, honestly. I probably wouldn't tell you. Don't give out information to random werewolves who wander in. But I'd think about it at least."

This little witch is getting on my last nerve, and I can feel my blood start to boil. I watch her turn back to her orbs, and know I need to interrupt, to get her attention back on me. "So, it's your shop now?"

She shrugs. "Seems so."

Now we're getting somewhere. I could go home and report to Celia that her trusted witch has apparently retired, but I want a solution for her. I want to have something to bring back.

Everyone outside of the four of us thinks Celia is the lucky one. That an accident of birth—that at some point we moved in the womb and she came out almost fifteen minutes before I did—made her a queen. That she took the crown, and that's something desirable.

It's been a burden on her. We all know it. And we all aim to reduce that in whatever ways we can.

And right now, that means solving this relatively minor border spell problem and keeping it off her plate entirely.

"I'm here with a job from Queen Celia of the werewolves," I reiterate. "Greta Snow did the spell for her for over a hundred years."

She doesn't even have the courtesy to look at me. "Look, I already told you. I can't find Greta."

"We'll pay well," I interrupt, and that makes her stop.

Chapter Four

Mae

*P*ay. *Money.* How much of my brain has been occupied by money lately?

Maybe this spell, whatever it is, was how Greta kept this place afloat. I definitely know it's not by selling crystals.

I huff a sigh. "Alright. What is this spell?"

A good witch will get all the terms on the table upfront. Like what exactly we'll pay well means. But also exactly what type of magic the queen is looking for.

If it's too specialized, it might be out of my wheelhouse. Witches aren't exactly great at sharing knowledge with each other. I've heard of genuine wars being fought over swiped spell books.

Greta was a little more generous than most, at least when it came to me. About half of what I know, she taught me. But I'd be stupid to think she taught me everything she knew. And I'm not stupid.

"It's our border protection spell," he says, and I just stare at him blankly, because that tells me next to nothing.

I can tell his frustration is rising, but he keeps his temper. He's doing deep breathing or something, I can tell. Maybe he does yoga.

I try to banish the image of the giant werewolf in downward dog. First imagined for its ridiculousness, my mind refuses to let it go for other reasons.

Hm. Interesting.

But no matter how hot the werewolf is and no matter how long it's been since I've gotten anything—this shop is a drain on me more than just financially—Greta always said you didn't sleep with customers, and frankly I don't think it's bad advice.

"It's always confused intruders, turned them around. Humans entirely, and most supernatural creatures too, unless they were invited."

Okay then. That's officially out of my wheelhouse. I don't even have an inkling of where to begin. Could not even guess.

But I keep my poker face on. No need for him to know that. Not when Greta left for her eternal honeymoon in such a rush that there's definitely spell books lying around.

Maybe she wrote it down. Maybe I'll be lucky.

"And how much are we talking about?" I ask, trying to keep my voice cool and even, like it's maybe interesting to me, like I definitely have this spell under control.

Then he says a number so large that I completely lose control of my poker face and ask him to repeat it.

But I hear the same thing. "Five hundred thousand dollars." Half a million. Enough to keep the shop afloat. And then some.

Yeah, this was definitely Greta's keep-it-together money, and I'm once again pissed she didn't think to leave any sort of information for me.

Just keep the shop running, Mae. Keep it away from Clay, Mae.

Fuck that. No "a very hot werewolf will come and offer you a cool half million if you do this spell, here's the steps."

That would be too easy.

"Alright," I say, doing my absolute best to pull my poker face back together. "Come back in two days."

He blinks at me. "Two days?"

"Two days." Enough time to tear this place apart and try to find the spell. Hopefully, enough time to cast it, although I wouldn't bet the farm on it. Big spells can take longer.

He looks like he's going to say something. Probably something rude. But what can he do? He needs me.

I just keep the poker face until he turns on his heel without so much as a goodbye.

And I pretend I don't watch him leave.

CHAPTER FIVE

BRYCE

The scent of magic fades enough when the door closes behind me that I can breathe again.

It's like it was choking me, honestly, cutting everything else off, and for an animal that relies so heavily on a sense of smell, the wolf did not like that.

I take a deep whiff now, trying to get my bearings back.

I pause, holding completely still. There's something in the air... no, back in the shop. Something I couldn't smell before, not through all the scents in there. Something that tells me I have to go back in. Now.

I shake my head to dislodge the stupid thought. Why? Just so I can argue with the witch again? That's the last thing I need.

That she was stunning puts it too mildly. With her flaunting her curves like that and her expressive eyes and pretty, smart mouth, I wouldn't mind seeing her again. But this is a job, and I don't fuck around with work. Not even for witches with smart mouths and fantastic tits.

Forgoing the cab, I walk down the street. I need a hotel and a meal to help me put the shop out of my mind. I have two days before I have to deal with that infuriating witch again.

I'm six blocks away before I realize I never even got her name.

***

I don't call my sister. I probably should. I should tell her that her pet witch is missing in action, and that I've found a replacement. A dubious replacement, to be sure. A pretty, tiny little thing who wears shirts I can see straight down.

But she's a replacement, and in two days I'll have the spell.

I don't call Celia. I can handle this one on my own.

***

The witch has hands as soft as silk.

They cup my balls, all gentle and seductive, and she looks up at me with a teasing smile. It makes my breath catch in my throat, my entire attention captivated by those sinful hands and that wicked mouth.

Her smile is painted red and I half-wonder if it would smear on my cock if she sucked me, if she'd leave behind a ring of red on me.

My cock jerks just thinking about it, and her smile widens.

"Want something?" she asks in a voice that carries all the sultriness and promise that I knew lay underneath the sarcasm from earlier.

There's a lot of answers I could give her. I want her to move her hand; I want her mouth. I want her to take off that corset top and show me what it's barely hiding, those plush tits highlighted deliciously by the black material, pushed up to a frankly alarming degree.

I wonder what it would be like to get my mouth on them. They'd overflow my hands as I grip them, squeeze them, raising them to my mouth, and—

She squeezes my balls, not enough to hurt, just enough to remind me she asked me a question. "Want something?" she repeats.

I growl, then grab her by the shoulders to haul her up to me.

She lets go of my balls, laughing as I manhandle her with ease. I'm so much bigger than her, absolutely dwarfing her, and I'm able to move her like she's a little doll.

She's straddling my stomach now, and I realize abruptly that it's not just her top that borders on indecent. She's wearing a skirt so short it's entirely rucked up around her hips now, her hot core pressing against my stomach and making me want to fill her. I bet if I touch her at all, I can get her to leak through those thin panties and leave a mess on my stomach.

I practically salivate at the thought.

She smirks at me again, one hand on my chest, right over my heart. "Want something?" she asks for a third time.

I want her, and I yank her down into a kiss to make sure she knows it.

***

I wake up with my hips humping nothing but air, a growl ripping through my throat. It takes me a long moment to place where I even am.

I'm in the hotel. The hotel I had to pay for because the damned witch is making me wait for the spell.

The witch. Just thinking about her makes my cock twitch again, harder than I've been in years. Dear gods, I'm close.

Without allowing myself to stop and think about it, I shove my hand down under the blankets, gripping my shaft and starting to stroke. My movements are quick and proficient, bordering on brutal. It won't take much to push me over the edge tonight.

Without my conscious input, my thoughts drift back to her. Those red, red lips. That curvy little body that has so much to give.

Her tits. Gods, her beautiful tits, looking so soft and full and absolutely straining that shirt.

I close my eyes and come, imagining I'm coming all over her chest.

I've started to think about what it would look like to watch my come drip down those spectacular breasts. I'd chase it with a finger, and—

I snap myself out of it. What the fuck am I doing?

She's just an annoying little witch. She technically works for me. And I don't even know her name.

Writing the top sheet off as a loss, I wipe my come-covered hand on it, then kick the blankets back so I can get out of bed.

My legs feel weak under me. Some witch who I haven't even touched isn't getting me this worked up. This is not happening.

Maybe I need to get laid. I've been busy lately and haven't made time for that in a while.

Well, I have time to kill here in New York, I think as I turn the shower on. I could take care of these urges.

And not with that damned witch.

CHAPTER SIX

MAE

I put the closed sign on the door as soon as I know he's gone.

I'd never lose a day of sales but, hey. A half a million dollars. It changes your priorities.

I know it won't work because I've already tried a dozen times, but I pick up one of the orbs I just enchanted and scry for Greta.

Nothing. Nada. Zilch.

I'm not the most powerful witch in the world, so maybe the problem is my own abilities. But my scrying orbs have always worked before. Greta taught me the enchantment herself.

Where the fuck is my cousin?

Not dead, I don't think, although honestly the evidence would absolutely lean that way for an outsider. Witch suddenly abandons home and lifelong business to go somewhere with a lover no one even knew she was seeing, and then drops off the face of the earth. Yeah. I've listened to true crime podcasts before; I know how it works.

But she's not dead.

For one thing, this shop still positively hums with Greta's magic. And while some of that will probably linger forever in her enchantments, there's more to it than that. Her life-force lingers in these walls. It'd feel different if she died, and that's that.

For another, if she died, I'm going to go find my great-uncle the necromancer and demand he raise her so I can kill her myself for sticking me with this shop forever.

So, no conveniently scryed Greta to give clues to this elusive spell. I have to do this the old-fashioned way.

There's two traditional ways for a witch to come up with a spell. One, experimentation, which has always been my preferred method.

Or two, shamelessly steal it from another witch.

And since I gave myself a two-day deadline, experimentation is off the table. So, raiding every inch of this place for anything Greta left behind it is.

***

The books are behind the damn refrigerator.

It's probably not even all of them. I'd found three lying around when I first moved in, but those had been minor spells, things that are either entirely useless to me or I'd learned my own ways of doing long ago.

There's four more books behind the fridge, and one quick pass-through tells me these aren't minor spells.

Jackpot.

Greta's spell books have always read like recipe books, which I've appreciated. Simple, straightforward. No messing around with ancient riddles or any of that nonsense.

I flip open the most promising of the books, expecting to find a neatly detailed spell. Ingredients, instructions, cook time, bam. Easy-peasy.

And it's not in English.

"Greta, you bitch," I mumble. "You're not old enough for this shit."

Greta, not even two centuries old, has somehow left me a spell book written in what I think is ancient Sumerian. I want to throw it out the window.

Only one of the four books is written in English, and a quick scan shows me nothing about boundary spells.

I pause for a moment, considering, but I know what I need to do.

She picks up on the third ring. "I have an ancient language problem," I tell her immediately.

It's silent for a moment. "Who is this?"

"C'mon, Ces, it's Mae."

Cesily and I dated two decades ago. We're amicable now. Mostly.

Well, the pool of witches in New York wouldn't be big enough if you never spoke to people you dated and split from, especially when it was decades ago.

Cesily sighs. "Hi to you too, Mae. I've been great, thanks for asking. The university is fascinating, yes. How have you been?"

Cesily is probably the smartest witch I know. A strong believer in the shamelessly steal other's spells approach, she's made a living out of obtaining different academic degrees so she can hunt down ancient spell books once thought lost to time. She doesn't exactly share them, but from what I know, she's doing alright at it.

Which means an ancient spell book written in a dead language? Right up her alley.

I'm going to have to show it to her, which means I'm going to have to share it with her, but that's a price I'm willing to pay. I need one spell in here, and it's worth half a million dollars and keeping Greta's shop for her, and I'll live with whatever else happens.

"I'm good, yeah," I respond to her absently. I am so far from good. I am whatever the opposite of good is. But here's a chance. I have to jump on it. "Look, I think it's Sumerian, but I have no idea. You know I suck at this. So... pretty please?"

I hold my breath. It might work. "I'm out of the country," she says.

"What?"

"C'mon, Mae. You know this is what I do. I'm on an excavation in Turkey. There's some good leads here."

Which means she thinks my spell book is crap, and not worth even attempting to translate. I try not to let it sting.

I take a deep breath. Cesily and I never exactly loved each other, but we'd fucked like it for a few years. There has to be enough lingering affection there for me to get through to her. "Please, Ces," I beg. "Listen, I have a commission for a spell that might be in these books. And this commission is the difference between saving Greta's shop and losing it. Please."

She's silent for a long minute, and I begin to think she hung up on me. "What do you care about Greta's shop?"

It's a valid enough question. I've known Greta my whole life. I learned most everything I know from her. And even with all that, even when Greta hadn't apparently been swimming in debt, I had never, not once, taken a job at the store.

Others probably thought it was just how territorial witches are, that Greta and I couldn't work in the same place. But the truth is, I just didn't want anything to do with the shop.

I love my magic. It's who I am, and I couldn't separate it from myself if I tried. But I never wanted it to be my job. My magic is for me.

"She left it to me," I tell Ces, hoping she understands. "And I'm not going to let her down."

She's quiet again for a moment, and I wait with bated breath. "I know someone," she says eventually. "I'll tell him to call you."

I'm so relieved it feels like I could float. "Another ex?" I manage to tease.

He could be my ex too, for all I know. The pool in New York really is small.

"Ces, thank you," I tell her, meaning it, hoping she knows it. "Can you tell him to call me quickly? Only there's a deadline, and—"

"Yeah, yeah," she says, and I can practically hear the eye-roll. The affection is over, apparently. "Listen, I'm due at the site in thirty minutes. I'll text him before I go." She pauses just a moment. "Be good, Mae."

"You too, Ces." She hangs up, and I stare at my phone, hoping whoever her person is comes through.

CHAPTER SEVEN

BRYCE

I hate this damn city.

Completely unable to get back to sleep after my rude, wet awakening, I dress and decide to take a walk. The moon will be full in a few more days, and it'll feel nice to be outside.

But then I remember that New York smells. The entire city smells like garbage and piss, and every time I walk by a subway grate, a scent of some earthy, rotten horror rises from the depths.

Gods dammit. I half wish I could shove something up my nose to block the scent.

I make a mental note to get the witch's phone number tomorrow, because when the spell needs to be updated, I am not coming back out here.

There are clubs still open, and I suppose something has to be said for the city that never sleeps. I make my way towards one, pay the cover, and walk inside, letting the venue wash over me. The scent is still overwhelming, but at least it's the rush of sweaty, lust-soaked bodies. Natural, and normal, even if none of the scents stick out to me as especially nice.

What I need is to find someone, I think. Anyone I can remotely tolerate. Someone I can take back to the hotel room and fuck this out of my system, so

I don't have to go back to the witch's shop tomorrow wondering what she looks like without her clothes.

I make my way to the bar, starting with a drink so I can contemplate the prospects around me.

I get served pretty fast for a place like this, and find a vantage point where I can survey the whole club.

A city like New York definitely has clubs for creatures like me, but I don't have it in me to put in the effort to find one. I try to separate the scents, see if any supernatural creatures have made their way here for the night. There may be a few, but their scents aren't especially distinctive, and separating them from the bodies around them is too much work.

That's fine. Humans are fine. I can be gentle, and it's not like I'll be so overcome that any of the more beastly parts of me will come out to play. I can control myself.

I sip my drink and survey the club.

She notices me about the same time as I notice her. Leggy, blonde, tall for a human woman. Everything the witch who I can't get out of my damn head isn't.

I try very hard not to think that she looks like a slightly more well-endowed version of Bethany, because thinking of Bethany, my sister in all ways but blood for a thousand years, in any sort of sexual context is a surefire way to ruin the entire night for me.

I let a slow smile slip over my face. Bait.

She takes it, making her way over to me.

"I'm Jess," she introduces, sliding right into my space.

Jess. She's been dancing for a while, judging by the slight sheen of sweat on her skin, and doesn't smell like she's had more than one drink. Her eyes seem steady, focused.

"Bryce."

"Nice to meet you," she says, and her teeth are blindingly white when she smiles. "Wanna dance?"

Not really, but saying actually, you wanna fuck seems rude. So I nod, extending a hand. "Lead the way."

She does, confidently dragging me to the dance floor before pressing right up into my space.

My hands drift to her hips, pulling her closer. She seems to like this, squirming even closer to me, until there's not an inch of space between us. This close, she helps block out the scent of all the others, and I can smell her, her sweat, the alcohol on her breath, the perfume she wears and the shampoo she uses.

And the wolf inside me, desperately raring for a little action a few hours ago, goes completely cold.

It practically turns its nose up at her.

There's nothing wrong with this human. She's not drunk. She smells clean. She's generally attractive. There's absolutely nothing the wolf should object to.

You don't get a say, you bastard, I think furiously, but the wolf doesn't let it go. It remains cold to her, and as much as I wish the wolf didn't get a say, I grow colder and colder to her, too.

Fuck. I want to tear my hair out.

No. I want to get laid. But apparently, that's not going to happen tonight.

I fake a phone call and smile apologetically at Jess, shaking my phone slightly to emphasize what the problem is, before I turn to walk away, walking straight out of the club.

Fuck it. I'm sure Jess will find someone better in five minutes, and if I don't walk off whatever the hell it is I'm feeling, I'm going to lose my mind.

***

I walk until long after the sun comes up, trying to burn away my pent-up frustration in the only way I can.

Eventually, I have to give up. I'm nowhere near my hotel, I have very little sleep, no idea when the last time I ate was, and the walking really isn't helping anything.

Just one more day. Tomorrow, I can go to the shop, make sure that witch has done the spell as promised, and high-tail it out of town.

I find a diner on my long walk back towards the hotel and make my way inside. Maybe food will help.

Food helps a little, because a hungry wolf is a bastard. So I devour two stacks of pancakes and eye up the pretty waitress pouring coffee.

The wolf in me likes the food, but remains completely cold to the woman.

Damn it, what is with me? At this rate, I'm going to explode.

I pay for my meal, leaving a significant tip to make up for the staring the waitress probably noticed, and make my way back to the hotel.

Maybe if I'm lucky, I can sleep the day away.

Chapter Eight

Mae

There's a pounding on the shop door at three in the morning.

To tell the truth, I probably wouldn't have heard it, given I'm an entire floor away and there's ambient noise from the city even at this time of night, but one of the first things I did when I moved in was set a spell on the door for exactly this purpose. So the minute the fist hits the wood, I get a little shock.

Magical burglar alarm. Handy.

Except if this is a burglar, they're the worst one I've ever seen. They're failing at the basic principles of breaking and entering.

Namely, the entering. With the force of their knock, I'm not convinced they haven't broken my door.

I'm halfway torn between opening my window enough to scream at them to get lost and going downstairs to see what the fuck is going on.

Going downstairs wins out.

It's not the smartest decision in the world. But if it's a drunk or lost human, or even one who simply is the worst robber in history, then I can deal with them. I'm a witch in a magic shop. I can handle stupid humans.

And maybe it's not a human. Maybe it's someone who desperately needs something from the shop and will pay through the nose for it.

I grab my robe and a vial of a powder I've spelled to cause massive, disorienting confusion—about as effective as a baseball bat blow to the head—and go downstairs.

"I'm coming," I snap as the knocking doesn't cease.

I get to the door and I see that it's not a drunk or a tourist or a robber or any other variety of human. But it's not a paying customer either.

I swing the door open, gripping the vial I took from upstairs tighter as I lean against the door frame, arms crossed over my chest. "What are you doing here?" I snap, fight or flight already activated at just the sight of him.

He smiles that slow smirk I had almost forgotten. "Not happy to see me, Mae?"

"Are people usually happy to see you?"

"And to think I came all this way to do a favor for you," he says, shaking his head.

I don't move out of the doorway, brain turning over what he's saying. It's three in the morning, so it takes me an extra minute before I figure it out.

"Ces sent you, didn't she?" I wasn't too far off the mark earlier then. Another former ex of Cesily's, although thankfully, this one is not one of mine too.

He smirks. "She said she had a favor you needed. Are you going to invite me in?"

I don't move from my place in the doorway, arms still crossed. I know I'm not an intimidating picture. I'm in my bathrobe. I'm five foot one on a good day, and he dwarfs me. But I don't back down. "Why on earth would I ever let you in here?" I say, trying to keep my voice cool and even, like maybe I'm just annoyed. Like all he did was disturb my sleep.

All I can think about is Greta's note to me. Witches don't give things to other witches. Witches hold things close and take everything else and never, ever give up what's theirs. But Greta gave me the shop. Maybe people like Violet and Ces think she just wanted to make sure her shop didn't die.

But I know what was on the last note she wrote to me: Whatever you do, keep Clay out.

"I can read whatever spell book you found. Whatever thing you found left by Greta is probably not worth much, but you know I can take a look as a favor for family." He tried to give me that charming smile again, and it feels like slime dripping down my back.

I've known Clay since I was born. He's never done anyone a favor in his entire life. He's not here for me or for Ces. Even if they broke up amicably enough for that to be a thing he'd do for her, I don't think he has it in him to do a favor. To care.

He's here for the spell book. He's here for whatever secrets Greta may have left behind for gods know what reason.

I wish it wasn't so early in the morning. I wish I hadn't just woken up and I wish I wasn't standing here in my bathrobe. I want time to think about what I'm going to do, but he's standing right in front of me and I can't exactly send him away.

He won't take it well and he won't come back if I let him leave. With Clay, he always has to have the upper hand. Always. And if I try to be in control here, I'll lose him.

Usually losing him would be my first priority, but I can't read those books.

I take a slow, shaky breath, uncross my arms, and step aside. "Come in," I grunt.

His grin makes me want to kick him back out—and maybe literally kick him—but it's too late. He's inside now, and he knows he holds all the cards here.

"Since when can you read Sumerian?"

"I assumed all clever witches would learn," he says, raising his eyebrow like it's so obvious.

I flush. I want to tell him to stuff it, but I bite my tongue.

He smirks like he heard it anyway. "Show me the spell books then."

I freeze. I don't want him upstairs. I don't want him any more in my space than I already let him. The shop is technically public, but the apartment is different. Before it was my space, it was Greta's, and Greta didn't want him anywhere near us.

"Wait right here," I say. I try to put as much firmness behind my voice as I can. "Don't move. Don't touch anything. Don't even look at anything. I'll be back in two minutes."

He makes a show of shoving his hands in his pockets. "I'll be right here," he promises.

Not trusting him an inch, I look over my shoulder twice as I go up the stairs to the apartment. I'd like to take the time to change, to wear something besides a bathrobe, especially when Clay looks like he just came off of a modeling shoot somewhere. But that would take time and time is the one thing I don't have.

I gather the spell books, leaving the one already in English upstairs. One less thing for him to get his hands on.

I'm sorry Greta, I think. But I have to choose between saving the shop and keeping him out and I am choosing your shop. I'll be able to get him out in an hour or so.

He's going to walk away with something. I know he is; even if it wasn't Clay and it wasn't his scheming, smarmy self, any self-respecting witch would demand something for the job. It's just the way we work.

I wonder what he could possibly demand. Access to the spell books, maybe, but I have a feeling it's more than that.

Whatever you do, keep Clay out.

True to his word for once, Clay is still standing exactly where I left him, hands still in his pockets. "What do you have for me?" he asks.

I plop the three spell books onto the counter and make a sweeping gesture with my hands, telling him to get to it. "Enjoy."

He meanders his way over to the counter but keeps his hands in his pockets and doesn't so much just look at the books. "Not so fast," he says, almost like he's scolding. "We're witches. Let's be honest—we both know what comes next."

I swallow. "Payment."

"Yeah. Payment," he says. "Something you must understand now, running a business and all." I don't think I imagine the sneer in his voice.

"What do you want?"

"To start?"

I debate saying I could have anyone here in an hour to translate. That I don't need him, that he can't make demands. But I'd be bluffing, and we both know it.

Clay wouldn't come all the way over here if he didn't already know he would win this little encounter.

"What do you want, Clay?" I ask again. I can hear how tired I sound, and I'm sure he can too, but there's nothing I can do about that.

He frowns. "Let's start with access."

"To the spells?"

"To the store. You already did so good, letting me in."

"Sorry," I say. "Not hiring."

"What do you want with this place, Mae? It's never been your style."

"What would you do with this place?" I challenge, leaning into him across the counter.

"A damn sight more than you."

Yeah, that's what worries me.

Clay's always had a dark side. A talent for darker spells. And Greta was probably right to worry about what he'd do if he had a location and a standing in the community to sell that through.

"I'll share the spells," I say, trying to make it sound firm. "That's all."

"That's the start," he insists. "And since I can read them and you can't, someone might argue that they're more mine than yours anyways."

"What else do you want?"

"I told you. Access. Invite me back."

Invite him back? What does that mean?

I shake myself. I can't go back and forth with him all day. I need these spells, or else there won't be a store to keep him out of. "Sure. In a week. And not at three in the morning. During business hours. You can come back for a visit."

He smiles, seemingly satisfied. "We'll talk then."

Asshole. He's going to string this along for as long as he can, and I'm in no position to argue.

I push the books closer to him. "Start reading. I'll get you a notebook for your translations."

CHAPTER NINE

BRYCE

I make myself wait until ten to go back.

There. Business hours, and not looking like I'm desperate to see the witch.

Because I'm not. I'm not desperate. I don't know her name, don't know anything about her.

I'm just horny as fuck with a stubborn wolf. That's it.

The little slip of a witch by the crystals is there again. I ignore them entirely, looking for my witch.

Not my witch. Dammit.

The argument with myself is pushed out of my mind entirely when I see her emerge from the beaded curtains leading to the back room.

She looks even shorter today, and I sweep my eyes over her to realize that the chunky heeled boots are slightly less alarmingly tall.

I really was just looking for why she's shorter, but I can't help taking in the rest of her as my eyes travel back up her body.

She has a skirt that's long and flowing and might even look conservative, but when she walks, I can see it's separated into multiple panels, with slits over her legs that go clean up her thighs, showing so much tantalizing skin. Her black top—if it can really be called that—exposes her entire midriff and barely contains her tits.

Just the sight of them sends me hurling back to my dream and the jerk-off session afterwards, and I dig my claws into my palm to force the thought away.

The pain helps. So does the strong smell of the place, the wolf in me curling his nose in disgust.

It's not that the magic smells bad necessarily. Witches don't repel wolves, and Chase's magic hasn't ever bothered me. There's just so much magic here, competing and overlapping, and it strips away every natural scent that I'd expect in a place like this.

Like hers.

I shake my head, forcing myself to focus. Talk to her. Get the spell. Go home and forget all of this.

I drag my gaze back up to her face, a little ashamed that I hadn't noticed before how tired she looks.

I clear my throat. Not my problem. I just need the spell, and then I'm out of here, and whether or not she's been sleeping will remain not my problem.

"Have you done it?"

She runs her hand through her messy hair and nods, not quite meeting my eyes. "Yeah, just finished it up. Should be good to go."

I narrow my eyes at the falsely cheery tone. Is she lying to me? Why would she lie to me? What purpose would she have in lying to me? If she lies to me, she won't get paid, and she should be smart enough to know she'll have the might of the werewolves after her. I look at her for a long, long moment, telling myself that I'm trying to determine what's going on with her and not simply lost in staring again.

She has beautiful eyes. She's doing everything she can not to meet my gaze, but even so, I can see her beautiful eyes. They're dark—almost black from this distance, although I wager they're brown up close—and they catch the light from the room around us, making them look like stars.

I tell myself to stop staring at her. Her eyes aren't that special, and I have better things to do. Still, it takes me a long moment to refocus. I dig my claws into my palm again, telling myself to move the fuck on and get the show on the road.

"Really?" I ask her.

She nods, a quick bob of her head that looks like she's trying to prove something to herself more than anything. "Really really," she says, with a layer of clearly fake cheer in her voice. "I just finished. All good to go."

I study her suspiciously for a moment, but what can I do? She either did the spell or she didn't. And she'd be an idiot to lie to me.

I'm big and I'm built and I know my way around a battlefield, and somehow I'm probably the least scary of my siblings. Even if she doesn't know us, she should know that much.

"We'll know soon enough, I suppose," I grumble. "All right. Payment will be sent upon confirmation." She nods. "I have to get home before I can confirm anything." It sounds stupid to my ears, just saying it, like I'm reminding both of us I have to leave.

"Sounds good."

I clear my throat again. What the fuck is happening with me today? Why can't I just hold a normal conversation around her?

There are business things to take care of, I remind myself. "I'm not mailing you a half million dollar check. I need your banking information so I can send you the payment."

She stops and blinks for a minute as if she hasn't considered how she's going to get the money. I know she wants it. I saw the look in her eyes when I brought it up the first time. How old is this witch? How unused to running a business like this is she?

"Alright?"

"Yeah," she says. "Of course. Just give me a minute."

"We could start with your name," I tell her. For purely business reasons, of course. Not because not knowing her name has haunted me since the moment I left her shop for the first time. "So I know who I'm even sending this money to."

"Mae," she says, voice barely more than a whisper. "Mae Yun."

I try not to let my brain get stuck on how it sounds. I want to say it. I want to let the sounds float over my tongue and into the world.

I stop myself. She's pretty and she's showing a lot of skin and she has a beautiful sounding name and something about her. That something makes me want to stare into her eyes a little bit longer, sure.

She also seems so young, and I'm paying her to do a job. I have to be professional here. I have to get my shit together.

I'm getting out of this town. The witch is off-limits. I need to leave as soon as fucking possible.

"Bryce Crae," I make myself say. It comes out more of a mumble than my usual smooth tone, just forcing myself to say something to keep the conversation going.

She looked me up and down. "Good to have a name to go with the face, I suppose."

I grimace. I can't believe I failed to introduce myself to Mae. Sure, I told her I was here on Celia's behalf, which is really the most important detail, but I didn't give her my name. Every single bit of politeness, every scrap of manners I drilled into my head, seems to have gone out the window with her.

As if that thought is its own temptation, my eyes drift down again to her exposed midriff, taking in the way the soft skin looks. I want to touch it. No, I want to bite it, and that thought is jarring enough that I force my eyes back up to her face.

I clear my throat. "Right. The sooner you get me the banking information, then the sooner I can wire you the money."

She gives me a shaky smile. "Coming right up."

Chapter Ten

Mae

Are all werewolves attractive?

There aren't really a lot of werewolves in New York. Probably something about the skyscrapers and the city streets really limiting their running around under the moonlight gig. So I can't say I've met too many of them in my life, but I have met a few and I don't remember them being as attractive as Hottie McWerwolf.

I might stare at his ass far longer than I should as he walks out of my shop. It's a delicious ass and I don't think anyone can blame me. The only person who might've seen is Violet, who has the decency not to look up from their crystal display. If they know what happened, then they're not going to mention it.

As soon as the wolf is completely out of my sight, I take a deep, shaky breath and retreat once again into the back. It's not like I have actual paying customers to worry about after all.

I let myself fall into a chair, running a hand over my tired face. I've barely slept since I met the werewolf for the first time.

I was up with Clay all night two nights ago, digging through the spell books, trying to find what I was looking for. It was made even more difficult by trying not to tip Clay off to what exactly I was looking for. I don't know what he would do with the information, but I still don't trust him as far as I can throw him.

All I know is, I could absolutely one hundred percent picture Clay trying to undercut me on the sale. Or worse.

How does someone corrupt a boundary spell? I'm sure with proper motivation, Clay could figure it out.

It doesn't matter. He'll be back in a week, and I'll have to deal with him then. In the meantime, I just have to hope the werewolf pays me. He could rip me off, I suppose. Maybe I'm incredibly naïve, but he doesn't seem the type.

Well, if he is, I'll just start spreading rumors that werewolves are cheapskates.

For now, my biggest concern isn't that they won't pay me. It's that the spell didn't work. It was long and complicated and I didn't get a lick of sleep and it took enough energy that I still feel a little bit of shaking in my muscles. Plus, having never done it before and not really having a way to test it, I'm not fully confident in my work.

But it is Greta's spell, and that gives me confidence. I read her notes in the margins, as vague as they were. The notes I could interpret on my own at least, and I didn't need Clay's help with those.

I wonder if I'll hear from the werewolf. I gave him my number, along with all that banking information, before he left. Maybe he'll call me to tell me how the spell worked. Or maybe a half a million dollars will just show up in the business account.

I shake my head and remind myself that yes, that should be my goal. This is about the damn money. I don't need some random werewolf I'll probably never see again, with a cute ass but a perpetually grumpy expression and who barely told me his name, calling me.

Violet pokes their head in through the beaded curtain. "You good in here?" they ask me.

I gave a shaky thumbs up. "All good." They look at me doubtfully, but at least they don't argue. Smart kid. Or maybe they're still just angling for a job.

Hey, with more half million dollar payments, maybe the job isn't that out of the question.

***

The week goes on as normal, except I double my stimulant spell intake in the mornings. The border spell really took it out of me, and it's almost four days before I feel like myself again. Still, other than additional stimulant spells, every day is the same old same old. Wake up, open the shop, have Violet come in and mess with displays but not buy anything, and tinker with the bigger things in the back.

I get a couple customers, some humans looking for their little occult witchy things, some more serious customers coming through to buy their things. And I even sell three of the scrying orbs, which makes it a pretty decent week overall.

But I can't relax. I can't settle back into the business. Part of that might be just how little I even like the business, but the bigger reason still lingers. Clay will be back soon and I have to figure out what he wants from me. More importantly, I have to keep him away from the shop. Greta was insistent that I can't give him a platform. I can't give him a foothold in the community that he can leverage and turn into selling his dark spells.

This is the one thing Greta did that I completely agree with. Sure, I'm pissed about pretty much everything else. She dumped the shop on me, left me with the financial burden, and did it all despite knowing I don't want it. But to keep it out of Clay's hands—I get it.

I learn to live with it.

I have to start thinking about how I'm going to handle Clay. What do I have to offer that's worth it to keep him out of the shop? But I don't have to think about it long, because the answer is nothing. There is absolutely nothing of value around here, and I know it.

As soon as the week is up, all I can feel is dread. We didn't set a specific time for him to arrive other than not at three in the morning, so I spend the day with bated breath, waiting for him to show up.

The asshole waits almost until the last minute, showing up at about five minutes before I plan to flip the closed sign. Clay knocks on the door, casual as anything, with a thick folder of papers under one arm and a smirk in place. "Miss me, cousin?"

I roll my eyes. "Like a wart."

"That's stereotyping against witches, you know," he says, smirk still in place.

I don't acknowledge that. Clay and I aren't in a place where we can tease and we really haven't been that for decades. Not for almost my entire life, really.

"What do you want, Clay?" I ask him. "Just to make sure we're all on the same page."

"You invited me into your shop tonight, correct?"

I swallow a bitter feeling, the desire to tell him *fuck no.* "Yes."

He makes a tut-tut noise. "No, no no. The whole thing, cousin. Please say it for the record."

I roll my eyes. He's always been a theatrical asshole. "I've invited you for this evening. Only into the shop, and only for tonight."

"Thank you. that's all I needed to hear." He pushes inside past me, walking in like that invite means he owns the place.

"What do you want, Clay?" I repeat, closing the door and flipping the closed sign before walking over to the counter.

He sets the folder of papers down on the counter in front of me. "Go ahead," he invites. "Read. It's in English, so even you can understand it."

I ignore the dig and flip over the papers with some trepidation. What the hell could Clay consider worthwhile enough to bring to me?

I don't understand all the legalese, but even I can understand what the papers say. They're for transferring ownership. They're for putting the shop in Clay's name. I look up at him, trying to hide the fury in my eyes. "The spells aren't worth the entire shop."

"From what you told Ces, they definitely were. You're in a terrible financial situation. Those books are probably actually worth more than the entire shop, financially speaking, at the moment."

I don't respond. It might be true. I haven't received my payment from the wolves yet, after all. "Nothing you tell me is going to get me to give you the shop, Clay."

He leans forward on the counter. "You don't want it, Mae," he says with a salesman's oily voice. "You never have. You and Greta like to think that we drifted so far apart, but I didn't forget either of you. Greta loves to shop. Loved, I guess, since she abandoned it, but it was her dream and never yours. It doesn't take a genius to figure that out. You've had two dozen dead end jobs in your lifetime. Maybe more, for all I know. I wasn't keeping that close track. Never once did you come here for work. Not when you were desperate, not when it could've been steady employment, not when you could stay here and not have to explain not aging to humans. Never once did you come here. You don't want the shop."

Everything he just said is absolutely true and I can't dispute it. That doesn't mean I'll give him the shop, though. It's Greta's shop, even now. It's Greta's shop and it won't be going to Clay. She was clear enough about that.

"The answer's still no, Clay," I tell him.

He stares at me intensely. "This is meant for both of us."

"Greta gave me the shop. She wanted me to have it. I'm not going to disrespect her wishes."

"What are you even planning to do with it? Make pennies selling charms to humans? Maybe you can sell magic kits! My first birthday magic kit with a little magic wand and a flower in a hat. I'm sure that wouldn't be a disgrace to your name as a witch," he sneers.

I force myself to keep eye contact with him, trying to keep him from seeing the truth. The shop is going under. The shop is a disaster. The shop is the last thing I wanted for myself, but none of that matters. Keep the shop away from Clay. That's all Greta asked.

I close the folder firmly, putting my hand on top of it, so Clay doesn't get any ideas about re-opening it. "If this is a favor for me, then I'm turning it down. I don't want it." I push the folder across the counter, back towards him. "So thank you but no thank you."

He takes the folder and I can see him failing to keep the scowl off his face. "This isn't over," he tells me.

Don't I know it. And don't I fear it. But it's over for now. I point towards the door. "Have a nice rest of your day, Clay." He turns and walks out, hiding his face and his reaction from me, but from the tension in his shoulders, I can see his anger, and I know that this has only just begun.

CHAPTER ELEVEN

BRYCE

"I'm telling you, he just walked in here," Callum says, body coiled with tension as he paces around the clearing he called me to.

There's an unconscious human on the ground. Probably not the smartest move, but I understand why Honor's instincts told her to attack the intruder. Besides, it's just so easy to knock a human unconscious.

I spare half a thought for the amount of work it'll take to deal with the human—someone will have to drive him outside of our perimeter, and drop him off somewhere safe, but somewhere he could have conceivably randomly passed out, and all before he wakes up—before turning back to the matter at hand.

"So, the border spell failed," I surmise. No use in thinking it could be anything else.

I look at the human again. A surveyor.

So not only do I have to help Callum fix this, but then I have to get back to getting the humans to leave our land the fuck alone.

And I have to hunt down a witch.

"Yeah, must have," Callum agrees. "I don't think that's ever happened before."

Me either.

We haven't always had a border spell, but when humans became a little more mobile, a little more enterprising, and a little more likely to have forgotten their fears of things that go bump in the night, it became a practical thing to have.

And Greta Snow had, from what I see, maintained that spell with precision.

And now, barely a week and a half with a new witch—a witch I found—the spell fails.

I ball one hand into a fist. This is on me. This is my mistake, and I'll fix it.

I turn to Honor, who's been hovering on the edge of the clearing. "Bring him somewhere," I tell her. "Make sure he's safe."

She nods, then swings the human up like he's a sack of potatoes, carrying him out of the clearing.

"What do we do next?" Callum asks, looking around at the stones that have always marked the boundary line for the village.

"I go handle a witch," I grumble.

Callum blinks, then looks me over. "Want me to go?" he asks, and I pretend I imagine the hesitancy in his voice.

Do I want him to go to New York, to find Mae? Do I want my brother, who just looks like a better version of me—hair just long enough to be a little roguish, a charming smile, laugh lines around his eyes—to go see my curvy, starry-eyed witch?

I haven't been able to get the witch off my mind. She haunts my dreams most every night still. When the full moon came, when I curled up in my home to avoid the frantically mating couples outside, my thoughts kept straying to her and her wicked mouth.

I need to get my head in the game. "No," I growl. "I've got it."

***

Flying to New York takes forever, leaving me room to stew in my anger.

Half a million dollars. That's what we paid her, just the other day. She scammed us out of half a million dollars for a spell that apparently has the life expectancy of a fly.

If she expects to get away with it, she has another thing coming.

It's well after business hours when I land, but I couldn't give less of a fuck. I get a cab and give her address, allowing myself to sit and steam as we make our way to the shop.

How dare she do this? How dare she think this was something she could get away with, that it wouldn't somehow bite her in the ass?

How young is this witch, anyway, to think she could do something so colossally stupid?

I pay the driver and slam out of the cab, walking to her shop door and, completely ignoring the little closed sign, begin to bang on it.

It takes over two minutes of banging. Just when I'm considering the merits of simply ripping the door off its hinges, I hear her. "Good gods, Clay, I'm coming! What the fuck do you want this time?"

I spare half a thought to wonder who Clay is. Maybe she's pissed off more than just the werewolves. Maybe she's on the bad side of multiple groups.

I don't allow myself to think about it too much, mostly because the wolf in me is furious at the very thought that someone could be mad at her.

I tell the wolf to shut the fuck up and bang on the door again, just to be contrary.

Mae pulls the door open with a surprising amount of force, leaving me with my fist raised. She stares at me for a long second, then props her hip against the door and crosses her arms over her chest.

I try not to stare. Try and fail.

"What the fuck do you want?"

Now my eyes firmly find her face, appalled she'd speak to me this way. Me, when I'm the one she screwed over. "Your damned spell didn't work," I grit out.

Her eyebrows shoot up and her mouth falls open. It looks genuine enough, but I remind myself that she betrayed me and to stop trying to give her the benefit of the doubt. "A week and a half," I continue. "Is that all your spell is worth?"

"No, it should have—" she trails off, shaking her head absently. "It should have worked."

"Well it didn't," I snap. "Should I take the money back and find someone else, then?"

The slight twitch in her eye tells me she doesn't have the money. Not all of it, anyway.

"No, I—I'll figure it out. I'll fix the spell," she says, and all the fight from a minute ago is gone. Her whole body droops, and I have to fight myself to not go and hold her up.

"What would make me believe it'd be any different this time?" I demand.

"Look, I—please. I'll fix it."

I look her over. I don't want to believe her. It'd be stupid to believe her, and if there's one thing that people can say about me, it's that I'm not stupid.

Begrudgingly, entirely against my will, I believe her anyway. There's something in her eyes that I can't quite resist. Desperation, yes. But something else too.

"You have twenty-four hours," I tell her. "And I'm not leaving town. If, in twenty-four hours, my brother can confirm that the spell is working, then I'll leave and we'll be fine. But if not..."

I let the threat hang in the air because I don't know how I'd finish it.

She gets the message, nodding slowly. "Got you. I'll see you in twenty-four hours, then."

She closes the door in my face, and I watch her through the glass until she's out of sight.

Chapter Twelve

Mae

"What the fuck did you do to me, Clay?" I demand over the phone.

He laughs dryly. "What makes you think I did something, Mae?"

I'm not in the mood to fuck around. It's well after midnight, I've been on edge since the moment Clay walked back into my life, and I've had a werewolf threaten me tonight. Not to mention, I had to call Cesily and beg for Clay's number, which is embarrassing.

"So help me, I'll—"

"You can't do anything, Mae," he interrupts. "Face it. You're powerless. And what limited power you do have is hobbled by that precious shop."

I grit my teeth. Witches like Clay and their focus on power. Just because I don't use my magic like he does, don't want to use it like he does, doesn't mean my magic is worthless.

"I will ruin your life," I threaten. I don't have any idea how I would do that, but I'll get creative. "I will destroy you entirely if you don't tell me how in the hell to fix that spell."

I don't know how he figured out which spell I was after. I probably gave it away somehow, seemed too eager.

"Why don't you just use Greta's charming annotations?" he asks tartly, confirming that he completely knows which spell I wanted.

"You're a fuck-head, you know that?" It's childish and I can't help it.

"Well, Mae, seems we're at an impasse."

"Just give me the proper translation."

"No pay, no play. Sorry, Mae."

"What do you want, Clay?"

"You know what I want. You already let me in."

"You're not getting the shop," I tell him.

"Then you're not getting a translation."

I'm glad he's not here in person. Because I'm convinced I'd absolutely strangle him right now if he was.

"What the fuck do you want with this place?" I demand. "It's a money pit. I literally cannot bring in enough cash to keep the doors open." "That sounds like a personal issue. Don't assume we're the same," Clay says. "I have friends. They have a business plan. Greta's shop, with the enchantments already on it, and the customer base built in, we could make money."

I hate everything about how that sounds. All I can think about is Greta's warning to keep Clay away from the shop.

"Sorry, Clay. No dice."

"Then no spell for you."

I close my eyes. The literal definition of being caught between a rock and a hard place.

Either way, I'm going to lose the shop. Either way, I'm going to disappoint Greta.

No. Turning Clay down was the one thing Greta asked for. I can stand firm on that, at least. And from there, I'll figure the rest out.

"Yeah, well. I'll live with it," I tell him, and then hang up so I can have the last word.

***

"You look like shit," Violet tells me in the morning.

Violet usually keeps to themself, but apparently this morning I warrant a comment. It's probably fair. I've already had four coffees laced with stimulant spells, way, way more than I'd ever recommend to anyone.

I didn't sleep at all last night, thinking about how when the werewolf returns, I'll have to explain that I can't do the spell. And then thinking about how I owe him half a million dollars, about twenty thousand of it already gone, spent on rent and Greta's debt and merchandise.

How the fuck am I going to make up that money?

"Feel it too," I tell them, slumping miserably against the counter.

Violet messes around with the crystal display for a moment, then walks over to me. "Here," they say, sliding a crystal into my hand. "Should give you some energy."

I look down. It's carnelian, but I'm pretty sure this one isn't even enchanted, just one we sell to humans who walk in off the street.

I clutch it anyway.

"So," Violet says, leaning more fully onto the counter to get comfortable. "Want to tell me what's wrong?"

I bite my lip. Violet and I aren't really friends. They're not even my employee.

What the hell else am I going to do? Call Ces again? Yeah, right.

"I'm only able to keep the doors of this place open because I sold a spell to the werewolves," I tell them. "They paid well. Only, I'd never done the spell before. It's Greta's spell, and I had to get it translated, and Clay butchered the translation to blackmail me, and now they're asking for their money back or for me to fix the spell and I literally don't know how and I—"

Violet cuts me off by taking my hand, still clasped around the crystal they pressed into it. The contact is so startling that I stop entirely.

Gods, when was the last time someone touched me? How pathetic is this?

"So the spell isn't going to work," they surmise.

"Not unless you know someone who can translate Sumerian. By, like, twelve hours from now," I agree.

"Yeah, not going to happen. But listen—a boundary spell. What would it take to do that?"

Something about Violet is honestly calming. I can't explain it. I look deep into their eyes as they try to get me to process what they're saying and take a deep breath.

Spells. Right. I can do this. I can think about spells.

Spells don't have to come from spell books. If they did, we'd all have killed each other fighting over them a long time ago.

No, spells can be made. Unique to the witch casting them, made for each witch's process. I know this. Greta taught me this, and I've done okay for myself over the years approaching my magic this way.

But that's for little things, like my stimulant spells. Or enchanting my clothes so I don't need to wear an ugly jacket during February. Or little good luck charms. Not a border spell meant to protect an entire village of werewolves.

"That's a big spell," I hedge.

"What would it take to do it?" Violet repeats.

What would it take for me to do it? A shit ton of magic. And time, probably.

"I'd need to be there," I say slowly, turning over the pieces in my mind.

"Probably."

My brain rushes ahead, tripping over itself to put all the pieces together. I'm going to the werewolf's home. I have to tell him that, and I don't know how he'll react. And I need to make sure the shop is going to be fine.

That part isn't too hard, at least. "Want a job?" I ask Violet.

They raise an eyebrow. "Is water wet?"

"Alright, well. Congratulations. You're on the payroll. Keep the shelves stocked, don't rob the register, and whatever you do, Clay stays out."

I can't afford to pay Violet without dipping into the werewolf's money. Well, I just won't take a salary. I'm already barely taking one, but I'll just go to nothing for a bit.

Maybe it'll all work out.

"Got it. Need me to sign anything?"

"What, like employment paperwork?" I have no idea if that's even something we have. I know Greta had employees over the years, but couldn't even guess how that worked for her. "Let's call this a trial basis," I suggest.

They look at me for a long moment, then nod. "Alright. I'll take over. You go pack."

***

I do pack. I have zero idea what's appropriate as a contract spell caster for the werewolves. I don't even really know much about where they live.

Whatever. I don't really stop to think what's appropriate to wear around New York, either.

Might as well go big. I find a body suit that really is more mesh than anything, a leather skirt, fishnets, and platform boots.

It's a statement. Humans look at me and think *witch*, witches look at me and think *amateur*, and no one ever knows quite what the hell is going on, but they're always staring. And I can work with that.

Then I have to wait for Bryce Crae to show up at my door, because the werewolf still didn't give me his number.

I pace the upstairs apartment while I wait. Gods, he's going to be in a pissy mood. I mean, he usually is. I haven't seen him non-pissy yet. And he always has that frown going.

It's kind of an intense expression. And I think he wants it to be mean, but it doesn't quite get there. Sure, he's aiming for mean. He's even tried to threaten me.

Something tells me he's soft underneath all that, though.

I just have to keep believing that, because I doubt he's going to be in a good mood when he shows up here today.

CHAPTER THIRTEEN

BRYCE

I call Callum when I get to a hotel room.

"You sure you want to give her another chance?" he asks, doubt clear.

"You know another witch who claims they can do the spell?"

"No, but I'm thinking we should work on finding one. I don't think yours is working out."

I let out a huff. He's not wrong. "This is a project for you and me. Keep Celia out of it." She doesn't need something else on her plate.

"Celia will be fine, Bryce. It's not your fault."

Callum doesn't understand. He never will. He's fifty years younger than us. He was never fourteen minutes from being the heir. He wasn't alive yet when Celia discovered what her destiny would be, the burden it would place on her.

Callum wasn't even twenty yet when Celia became the queen. Still a child, really. He'll never fully remember it the way Heath and I do.

Callum would give anything for this family. We all would. But Celia's had to give more than anyone.

I don't think the fuck up with Mae—with the witch, I correct myself—is my fault. But I think it's a fuck up, and we'll take on the burden of that.

Callum is quiet for a long moment. "What are you going to do if she fails again?"

I open my mouth to say a lot of things—kill her for screwing over the wolves. Hurt her, maybe. Make her suffer.

None of it comes out, and the thought of it makes me uncomfortable deep in my bones. "I'm hoping we don't need to find out."

That's all I can offer. Because against all odds, I'm rooting for the little witch. And not just because her getting the spell right is one less thing for me to worry about.

***

Her lips are a tantalizing red as she smiles at me, turning her head just enough to tease me, to tell me she's paying attention to me. But I catch the mischief in her eyes, and I want that attention on me entirely.

I grip her waist tighter, feeling the soft skin under my hands. She's wearing a button-down shirt that's completely unbuttoned. My shirt, I realize with a jolt of heat through me. And her skin is completely exposed under it.

She must feel how hard I am for her, perched on my lap like she is. I palm her breast, letting the heavy weight of her tit fill my palm. I want to suck it, want to kiss and bite at the skin there, want to see what moans I can draw from her, what will make her crazy.

Maybe she can read minds, because she turns in my grasp, planting her knees precariously on either side of my thighs. My hands automatically move to her waist to steady her, and she smiles that wicked red smile at me, her hands moving to my chest.

"Want something?" she asks.

And then I wake up.

***

I'm hard as steel in the hotel bed, completely alone and yet somehow still feeling a generously curvy witch in my lap.

Nothing for it. I roll, snaking my hand down under me to grip my cock. I fuck into my fist, pretending I'm fucking into her, and I come embarrassingly fast.

Then I get up, clean up, and sit on the edge of the bed.

It's not like I don't have a routine for this well at hand now. These dreams only haunt me almost every night.

That thought strikes something in me. Haunt.

Could this be some damned spell?

Why the hell would she do something like that? What could she think she could get out of it?

I growl. I mean to find out.

***

I don't wait the full twenty-four hours before going back to the shop. It's unfair to her, but I'm in a less than charitable mood.

The little witch whose name I still haven't gotten is at the register. That's fine. I go to push past them, heading for the beaded curtains.

They stop me with a hand on my chest and a look in their eyes that promises fire and brimstone.

I could pick up this little witch and break them in half. But I stop.

"She's not back there," they say. They have a very quiet voice, but there's an undeniable command under it. "She's upstairs."

I grunt. "Great. I'll go get her."

Quicker than I would think possible, they maneuver around me to block my way to the stairs. "You'll do no such thing. For one thing, I don't even think they'd let you up."

Let me up?

Damned witches.

"I will get her," they continue. "You'll stay here. Don't touch anything."

They hold a lot of anger towards me. I almost ask if they know their boss screwed me and my family out of half a million dollars. But they're gone before I can say anything.

I keep my hands to myself, feeling foolish standing in the middle of the empty shop, and wait.

Mae follows the witch back down the stairs. She's carrying a big duffel bag, and walking very smoothly considering the giant platform boots she's wearing, and that she doesn't look like she slept any better than I did.

"Good, you're here," she says.

I blink. That isn't quite the reaction I expected from her.

"Can we talk privately?" I ask her. I want to deal with whatever this dream thing is before I have to deal with the success or failure of the border spell.

She raises an eyebrow. "Sure thing. Violet, we'll be in the storeroom?" she says, sounding more like a question after a quick look at the beaded curtain.

I follow her through, and then follow her into what is little more than a glorified closet, filled with boxes of presumably magical items.

She looks around for a minute. "Someday one of us will have to organize this mess," she mutters.

"Can you control dreams?" I demand.

She blinks at me a few times, seemingly trying to catch up to my train of thought. "Not that I know of," she says, slowly, as if working through a puzzle. "I'm sure there is a spell for it of some sort, but I don't know it." She shrugs. "We sell a crystal that's supposed to give you good dreams?"

Good dreams? Is that a euphemism?

Because being very honest with myself, I can acknowledge that those are some good dreams.

"Why? You need me to control someone's dreams?" She looks at me shrewdly. "Or do you have a dream problem? Nightmares?"

Nightmares? Not exactly.

The thing about it is she seems to be telling the truth. Her dark eyes have absolutely no guile in them, and I haven't detected any of the usual indicators a person is lying.

Then again, with all the magic in this damn place, I can't smell anything, never mind the slightly sour sweat of a liar.

Even knowing that, I decide to believe her. I can't explain it, but I can't look at her and truly believe she did anything to deliberately hurt me.

So these dreams are mine then. Just mine.

It doesn't help me come any closer to understanding them.

"Anyways," she drawls, "Back to the matter at hand?"

Right. The border spell. The spell I came here for. That matter at hand.

"I need to come do the spell in person," she tells me.

"What?"

She shrugs. "Sorry. Look, it's a long story. And I'm not going to lie to you, I know it doesn't make me look good. But I'm relatively confident I can fix it, if I go in person."

"I don't like relatively confident," I say automatically, because it's expected, because I should push her.

She takes a deep, shaky breath and looks me square in the eyes. "If I can't do it, I'll give you your money back. All of it."

I know that hurts her. I know she doesn't have all the money.

Fuck it. What do we have to lose? And what other option do I have, anyway, other than to hunt for another witch?

That'll take time, and I suppose I can use that time letting Mae give it a try.

And deep down, some part of me thinks she can do it.

She hefts her bag up. "I'm packed."

I nod sharply. "Alright. Let's go. We'll book tickets at the airport."

I turn to leave, and she follows me out. She's seemingly ready to go, because all she does is tell Violet that she'll call to check in. Violet hands her a rock, and then Mae walks to the door, waiting for me to catch up.

I follow along behind her. "Let me carry that," I mumble, automatically reaching for her bag before I can even think about it.

She raises an eyebrow at me but hands the bag over, using her free hand to push the shop door open.

"I'll get us a cab, but honestly they don't usually stop around here, might have better luck if we walk two blocks over, and—" She's getting further away from me as she walks. Further away from the shop, with the door closing behind us.

That's when I smell it.

It's so sweet, so strong, so damn powerful. I can't believe I missed it before. But as soon as the scent from the shop is closed out, all I can smell is *her*.

And it nearly drives me to my knees.

Chapter Fourteen

Bryce

I gape at her, even as I inhale sharply, over and over, taking deeper and deeper draws of air. Her. Gods above, she's the sweetest scent I've ever experienced.

The wolf in me agrees, and I realize the wolf must have known the whole time. Even when that damn shop made it too difficult for me to figure it out.

"Hey? Hey, Bryce?" she calls, still a half dozen paces ahead. "What's up, man?"

I close the distance between us in a second. "Did you know?" I demand, my voice coming out far rougher than I intended it to. "Did you?"

She blinks rapidly and shakes her head as I level accusations at her.

"Know what?" She takes a deep breath. "What the fuck just happened?"

"That you're my mate."

She freezes completely still for a moment before taking a step back. "That I'm your... what the fuck does that even mean?"

I take a deep breath, trying to center myself and calm down. It actually works, not in the least because I get a big whiff of her scent.

Gods, I want to surround myself with that scent. Drown in it. Now that I can smell it, it's all I can think about. And I can't believe there was anything on this earth strong enough to keep it from me.

"I'm yours," I tell her, struggling to find the words to explain the bond that wolves just understand. Heath mated with an outsider, but Chase had understood the mating bond as well as any wolf would. I wrack my brain, trying to think of wolves who bonded with outsiders. I need their advice.

But for now, I have a completely confused witch in front of me, standing on the sidewalk in the middle of Canal Street, and I need to make this clear quickly.

"I was made for you, and you for me," I say, trying to watch her reactions. Her eyes are wide, disbelieving, and she's taken another big step back, which the wolf hates.

"And why the fuck would you think I would know about that?"

"I couldn't smell you. In the shop—it's like I couldn't scent it on you. I should've been able to scent it on you."

Her shoulders slump, something like defeat crossing her face. I immediately want to go to her and cheer her up.

Gods, everything makes so much sense now. The dreams. The extra chances I gave Mae, when I know full well I'd never give anyone else the chance to hurt the pack twice. The way I looked at her, couldn't stop looking at her.

The way I want to cheer her up. Hold her. Even right here in the middle of the street.

"Look, I don't know—I don't know what gave you the impression that I'm, like, super powerful, but I am very, very average," she says, looking somewhere over my shoulder instead of at me. "I can't control dreams. I can't do anything to make a werewolf not sense their mate, or anything else related to their mates, for that matter. The only reason I even suspected I could do the boundary spell is because I figured Greta left it in a spell book somewhere. I'm just average. I do my small magic and I like it, okay? I didn't do jack to you."

"Okay," I repeat back to her, trying to make my tone soothing as I take a small step forward, trying to close the gap between us. "Alright, Mae. I believe you." And I do. I, skeptical Bryce Crae, immediately believe her, no questions asked. "Must just be all the magic. Most wolves don't spend that much time around that much concentrated magic."

She shrugs. "Greta was way more powerful than I am. Wouldn't be surprised if some weird shit lingers in those walls. Now. Can we please go back to the I'm your mate shit? What the fuck does that mean?"

I have enough presence of mind to cast an eye around. The sidewalk isn't crowded, but there are enough people around, and I don't doubt that we've drawn some attention. Even in New York, where everyone seems determined to mind their own business, we would look strange.

"Not here," I say, trying to convey our audience with a flick of my eyes.

She gets it. "C'mon," she mutters. "I know a place."

And, as I'm realizing I'll do for the rest of my life, I follow her.

CHAPTER FIFTEEN

MAE

Mate.

What. The. Fuck.

On autopilot, I lead him over to Columbus Park. It's not the greatest solution, but I scope out a bench that's more out of the way than most.

Bryce sits next to me immediately, carefully setting my duffle that he's still carrying on the bench. The bench, not the ground. Because he wouldn't want to get my stuff dirty.

Of course, with the bag and my big hips and his big everything, there's not much room on the bench. Bryce solves this by sitting practically thigh-to-thigh with me.

"What is a werewolf mate?" I ask him.

"You don't know many werewolves, do you?"

"No. You guys don't tend to like the city. Now answer the damn question."

He's quiet for a moment. "Never had to explain it to anyone before," he says before he answers. "The wolf in us can sense it. A partner who's perfect for us, who we're perfect for. We dream about it our whole life. And the wolf will eventually help you find that person."

"And I'm yours?" I ask skeptically. Right. Like this wolf who seems to have his shit together would be the perfect partner for me.

Because other than a little attitude problem—and really, I understand I met him under stressful circumstances—Bryce Crae seems pretty great. He works for the werewolf queen. He travels. He's hot as hell.

What is he doing with a sixty-year-old witch who's never left New York, who begrudgingly manages a failing business, and apparently can't work the spell he hired her to do?

He winces, and doesn't that make me feel like shit? But then he says, "I know I didn't make the best first impression. We should talk. It's good that you're coming with me. We'll get to know each other. I promise, the second impression will be better."

That is not what I expected him to say at all. I take a deep, deep breath. "Look, you've got an attitude, but who the hell am I to judge that? You've heard me talk. You've met New Yorkers; we don't exactly back down from attitude. It's not the attitude itself. But I didn't get the impression you liked me much. And now—"

"I liked you far more than I thought I should," he interrupts. "Trust me. I'm a grumpy bastard, Mae, you deserve to know that up front. And if you come with me, everyone will tell you anyway. And I was here on official business. I never mess around on official business. I couldn't understand—my brother couldn't understand—why I gave you a second chance. Now I do."

None of this sits right with me. None of this feels right. He, what, smelled me a bit and now suddenly, all my sins against him are forgiven?

Is this a sex thing? Does werewolf mate mean he's just really horny? Is he suddenly being all accommodating because he just really, really wants to get laid?

Because, I'm going to be honest, I could be down for that. It's been a while, and Bryce is easy on the eyes, and seems like he has a type of intensity that could be fun. But nothing he's saying makes it seem like it's just a sex thing.

"I don't want you to give me a second chance just because you think I'm your mate," I tell him, studying my hands intently instead of making eye contact. My nail polish is chipping. "I want you to give me a second chance because I said I'd do the job, and I fucked up with the bad translation, but I do genuinely think I can do it this time."

He reaches out and takes the hand I'm watching, and I go entirely still. "This okay?" he asks, and I appreciate that he noticed enough to check in, even if I don't know what the hell to say. So I just nod. "I'd decided to give you the second chance before we left your shop," he reminds me, his voice more gentle than I've heard it yet. "Before I knew. And now I'm doubly glad. We'll have plenty of time to talk and figure this out when we're at home."

Home. His home. Hopefully, that's what he meant.

"You know mates that you know by scent are weird to the rest of us, right?"

"Not all of us. Demons have mates. So do vampires. Some other species too, I'm sure."

"Yeah, well. Most of us. Weird that you can sniff out a person supposedly perfect for you."

"I know. I'm sorry I don't have a better explanation. I don't know how to explain it or how to help you understand it. My sister mated a wolf, my brother mated a demon. They both just understood." He gives me a look so incredibly earnest that I squirm away from it a bit.

I get a feeling we're on two entirely different playing fields here. He's talking about commitment. Real, forever stuff.

I'm talking about keeping Greta's shop open, maybe getting fucked some time this decade, and maybe—in some distant, unrealistic world—kicking the stimulant spell habit because I'll finally have a proper sleep schedule. We are not on the same page right now.

"We can talk?" he offers. "We'll figure it out together. After all, we have time. You're coming to the village. And I'll answer any questions you have."

I'm not even sure I want answers. But the look in his eyes is so sad it's frankly almost pathetic. "I'm coming with you," I tell him. "I said I'd do my best to do this spell and I will. And we'll talk." Because whether or not I want answers, I have a feeling I'm going to demand them, anyway.

He nods quickly. "Of course. Whatever you want." He sounds so earnest when he says it that it makes me shiver a little.

Talk about a one-eighty. Whatever I want, huh?

"I want to get this job done," I tell him. At least I know that for sure.

He jumps up and offers me his hand. "Then let's go."

And then he takes my bag and leads the way out of the park.

***

"So," I ask him casually as we climb out of the cab at the airport. "Is this, like, a sex thing?"

He freezes for a second, then turns to fully face me. "Why? Do you want it to be a sex thing?" He offers me an almost roguish smile, and it changes his whole face.

His face was attractive before. Even the scowl looks good on him, honestly. Some good bone structure, there. But with the smile...

"Am I supposed to pretend you're not hot?"

"Not at all. It can be as much of a sex thing as you want," he promises me.

"So, you've thought about me that way? Before or after you realized I was your mate?"

He gestures me through the door into the airport, waiting until I'm walking right past him to say, "Both. Plenty."

Oh.

I make it through the ticket line in a kind of fog, wondering about the ethics of sleeping with the hot werewolf when we both clearly agree that the other is sexually attractive, but he also clearly wants far more out of this than I do.

After we have tickets—which Bryce pays for, and I spare half a thought on whether I should feel bad about that when I'm technically already half a million dollars in the hole with him—we go over to security.

My boots have zippers and are easy to remove, thankfully, although I'm three inches shorter when they're off. Never has my lack of height been more obvious than when standing next to a giant like Bryce Crae.

The TSA agent gestures at me. "Jacket too, honey."

I want to argue that it's a shirt, not a jacket, but even I know arguing with the TSA gets you nowhere. So I take off the bulky button-down, leaving me in just the bodysuit that barely covers my nipples.

And I feel Bryce's eyes on me the entire way through security.

He grabs my bag off the belt, then hands me my shoes while I put the shirt back on. He's still staring, eyes practically glued to my tits.

It's nice, honestly. To see how much they get his attention. And if he hadn't dropped the bomb that he thinks we're fated mates for life, I'd be really, really flattered.

Now, it just feels like something I can't deliver on.

He clears his throat and brings his attention back to my face after I do up a few of the buttons. "That's, uh…"

"What, people didn't wear stuff like this when you were born?" I ask. "How old are you, anyways?"

I sit on a bench to slip my boots back on, and he stands over me in a way that should feel intimidating but somehow doesn't.

It feels like he's my bodyguard. My big werewolf bodyguard.

"A thousand, or thereabouts," he says after checking to make sure no one is listening. But this is JFK. No one gives a fuck what anyone else is up to. "You?"

"A thousand? Gods, do you know what robbing the cradle means? I'm sixty."

His eyes seem to almost bug out of his head. "Sixty?" He flounders for a minute and I force myself to turn back to zipping up my boots. "I knew you were young, but sixty?"

"How'd you know I was young?" It's not like looks are a good indicator. He doesn't look that much older than I do.

A thousand. Good gods.

He gestures towards me, and I take it he means my outfit. "What, did they not dress like this in the literal middle ages?" I snark.

I know the look is a lot. I know I lean hard into the modern witchy, slutty goth stereotypes. Mostly, I like the reactions, like the irony of actually being a witch and dressing like this. Mostly, I like the way people look at me.

I really, really liked the way Bryce looked at me a few minutes ago. But if he's going to judge now…

"No, they didn't. And I'm very thankful for the more modern look, trust me." His eyes dip to the edge of the bodysuit he can see peeking out above my shirt. "Do you have anything warmer?"

"Worried people will think you're mated to a slut?" Oh, that sounded a little more biting than I intended.

He looks at me for a long moment, but he doesn't seem angry. If anything, his eyes seem to go softer again, completely ruining whatever I was about to say. "Worried you'll be cold, Mae. It's cold at home. Trust me, I am not complaining about your clothes." His eyes dip to my chest again, then down to my fishnet-covered legs. "But if you are cold, we'll find you something."

Oh, then. The wind goes out of my sails.

The thing is, I like when people look. And I am good at ignoring the comments, whether from my mother or the witch community or random humans on the sidewalk.

I'm comfortable enough with what I want and who I am to let the comments roll off my back. But somehow, the idea that Bryce would look down on me hurt.

But his eyes are hungry, not judging. And some stupid part of me wants to part my shirt and let him look his fill.

"I enchant my clothes," I admit. "It gets cold in New York too, you know. I can't be cold with these on, even if I was standing in six feet of snow."

He raises an eyebrow. "Impressive. And that's a little spell?"

I shrug. "For me it is." Every witch categorizes what's little to them differently, I suppose. Some things come easier to some people. But I'm not going to pretend I'm any great power.

He smiles at me again, and it's just as blinding as last time. "Impressive," he repeats, and it sounds like he really means it. "Now, if your shoes are on, boarding is in twenty minutes."

I stand up, and before I can even reach for my bag, Bryce takes it again. "But the ticket says the flight is still an hour away."

"Yes, but boarding is always—have you never been on a plane before, Mae?" he interrupts himself.

I suddenly feel small. He's the ancient one. He's literally older than most everything I can think of. I was born after the invention of the airplane, and somehow I'm the one who's ignorant here. "Never," I admit. "I've always wanted to, though." What an understatement.

He smiles again. "Well, let's do that, then." And then he leads the way to the gate.

Chapter Sixteen

Bryce

My head is spinning just from being around her.

For one thing, her scent is driving me crazy, making me want more desperately. I want to unpin her hair from the elaborate twists she has it in and bury my face in it. Want to smell her neck, her gorgeous thighs. Want to figure out what she smells like when she's happy, when she's excited, when she's coming.

And that's the mating bond driving me. But even outside of that, she's taking over my mind. Her clothes make me salivate, and I would give just about anything right now for her to take off that overlarge shirt and show me that almost transparent, skin-tight undershirt again.

On a less sex-obsessed level, every word out of her mouth is like a puzzle I'm ready to solve. My pretty little mate, barely sixty and has never traveled outside of New York but wants to.

Suddenly, every time I've complained about traveling fades from my mind. What would it be like to travel with her at my side? To get off the plane and not worry about what work the job will bring, but rather watch her take it all in?

Seeing places with her eyes will make it all worth it. It'll be all fresh and new, and I'll cherish every moment.

And it feels right that the first place I'm taking her is home.

My home. Hopefully her home, too, although I'm not stupid enough to think that everything will go smoothly. She has that damn shop she cares so much about, after all. And she hasn't mentioned family, but she's only sixty. Surely she still has family in New York.

But it will be her home. I'll spend every minute of the trip showing her why she should want it to be.

She really has never flown before. I put my hand on the small of her back, trying to steer her through the boarding procedure in a way that hopefully won't draw attention to her lack of knowledge. I get the feeling my mate gets embarrassed about things like that.

And, this way, I get to touch her. Even through that shirt.

If she's going to cover up that beautiful skin-tight, practically see-through undershirt, then she can do it with my shirts in the future. Just the thought of it makes my cock twitch, of her wearing a sexy top just for me, hidden underneath my shirt.

Once we're on the plane, I hoist her bag into the overhead compartment, gesture her into the window seat, and then do something I've never done on a plane before: I willingly take the middle seat.

Technically, her ticket is the one with the middle seat assigned, but there's no way in hell I'll let that happen. It's her first flight and she should get to watch out the window. And I don't want any strangers in her space.

I mean it as a kind act, but I'm also well aware that letting strangers be in the space of my mate would drive me practically feral right now.

I'm too big to be here, so I lean into Mae's space a bit, trying to give the woman in a full business suit and large chunky headphones on my other side some space. Mae looks over, like she might want to argue with me, but then she sees why I'm so close to her, and lets it go.

I take her hand like I did earlier, marveling at how small her fingers are in mine. These hands haunted my dreams, but the reality is somehow better.

I didn't remember the chipped black polish in my dreams, and it's somehow such a charming detail. I wonder if her toes are painted too.

She has scars on her hands, little nicks and cuts she must have gotten before she grew up into her immortality. There are stories there, and I relish the thought of her telling them to me.

We have eternity for her to tell me. And I'll tell her anything she wants to know, too.

She lets me play with her fingers as she watches out the window. I glance out, but immediately look away. They're just finishing loading luggage. And anyway, no matter what was going on outside, it wouldn't be half as interesting as Mae.

I have a lot of work to do. I know it.

That's okay. No one ever believes I can be charming, but I prove them wrong time and time again. This will just be one more time.

Mae watches takeoff with rapt fascination, but once we reach cruising altitude and get walled in by clouds, she loses a bit of interest. I watch as her eyes droop.

Good. This is the short leg of our journey, but she should get all the sleep she can. She still looks tired.

Probably over the spell I berated her about, I think grimly.

I let go of her hand to wrap my arm around her shoulder, using my other hand to shove the armrest between us up so I can tug her gently into my side. "I'm a comfortable pillow," I offer.

She snorts and jabs me in the rib with two fingers. "You're hard as a rock."

I bite back my retort that other parts of me can certainly be hard too, if she wants to find out. We're on an airplane filled with people, I have to remind myself.

"I'm better than the window."

She looks at me for a long minute, her eyes calculating. I don't know what she's thinking, so I just wait.

"I probably won't be able to sleep," she says eventually, but then, to my absolute surprise, just leans into my side, her head on my chest.

I wrap my arm around her a little more securely and trace light patterns on her arm. And, within five minutes, I feel her heartbeat slow and her breathing even out with sleep.

***

According to the little TV in the back of the seat, we've been flying a little over an hour when the first rock of turbulence hits.

The clouds outside of the window have grown darker and darker, and apparently we're not going to be able to out-fly this storm.

Mae wakes up instantly, the hand that's migrated to my chest grabbing at me. "What is it?" she mumbles, face still pressed against me.

I move my hand from her arm to her hair, stroking it. "Just a storm, Mae." But the plane rocks again, and her grip on my shirt tightens.

"Is this normal?"

"Normal enough." I keep playing with her hair. I'm messing it up, but she hasn't said anything yet, and I'm selfish enough not to stop. "What, you can't control the weather?"

That has the reaction I want. She looks up at me. "Are you serious?" But she sees my smile and just huffs. "You really have no idea what we actually can and can't do, huh?"

"You're telling me you don't know anyone who can control the weather?"

She just shakes her head and leans against me again, turning her face into my chest as the plane rocks again.

"Ladies and gentlemen, this is your captain speaking. We're currently trying to get you out of this storm, but we've just received word from the ground that our flight pattern is being diverted until the storm clears the area. If you have connecting flights, see a gate agent on the ground to rebook them."

Great. That means us. There already wasn't much time between our two flights, and now we're practically guaranteed to miss it.

Another jolt of the plane pushes Mae deeper into me. On second thought...

This is perfect, actually. I keep playing with her hair and think maybe the gods are looking out for Mae and I after all.

Chapter Seventeen

Mae

Planes are not as fun as I thought they'd be, and I think for a genuine moment that I might never want to get on one again.

Sure, we all land safely, and Bryce assures me this isn't an entirely abnormal occurrence, and it turns out having a giant werewolf teddy bear helps the whole experience. But turbulence? No thanks.

Of course, I can't exactly swear off planes entirely, because we now have tickets for the last leg of our journey for noon tomorrow. Lucky me.

"Are you good with room service?" Bryce asks me, once again holding my bag and placing his free hand on the small of my back. He has incredibly long legs, and it's only all my years practicing walking on crowded New York streets that allow me to keep up with him. "I'll find a restaurant if you want one, but this way, I figured, we could talk."

"Room service? When'd you get a room?" I ask. He was on his phone while we waited to talk to the gate agent, but I thought he was texting someone, not booking a hotel room.

Honestly, I hadn't even started to worry about that yet.

Sure, Mae. Nice one. Relying on the guy who I already owe half a million dollars to sort out food and lodging.

"Haven't gotten it yet. But if the airport hotel is full, we'll get a cab and look a little further out. Not worried, little witch."

Little witch. It sounds affectionate when he says it like that.

Honestly, I'd prefer him being an asshole again. At least we both one hundred percent understood where we stood then.

"So, room service?" he prompts. "Speak now or forever hold your peace, because we're walking right by all these restaurants."

"Room service is fine." It's only after I say it I realize it's not fine, because room service is going to encourage him to want to talk. To talk about the things we can't say in a restaurant. And that's just inviting too much intimacy into this.

But then again, I'm traveling to his home, where he lives. To a town full of werewolves that he can say anything he wants in front of. It's not like I can really avoid these conversations forever. And it's too late to change my mind now, not if I want to look like I have any sort of self-control.

I'm lost in my thoughts, and suddenly there's a sharp pain in my ankle and I'm tipping forward, the ground completely going out from under me.

Strong hands catch me before I can even panic. Bryce hauls me upright and pulls me to him, one arm banding across my middle as if I'll disappear if he doesn't hold me close, and it's only then that I even realize what happened. "Watch where you're going," he snaps at some middle-aged lady with a rolling bag.

She rolls her eyes at him and turns away, and Bryce actually growls a bit. "Easy there," I murmur. Gods, I feel completely surrounded by him. And he's been talking about scents all day, and I've already told him it's weird. But I've been noticing since the plane that he smells pretty good himself, honestly. "I'll survive an attack from luggage." I try to lighten the mood.

He doesn't let me go. "How's your foot?"

"Fighting fit, I promise." Like a rolling suitcase is going to be what takes me out.

"Let me see it." He's already steering me to a nearby chair, gently shoving me into it before he goes to his knees in front of me and grabs at my boot.

I stop him with a hand on his shoulder. "Bryce. I heal exactly as fast as you do. You don't need to stress about me getting clipped by a bag."

He has the decency to flush. "New mate thing," he murmurs, still holding my boot in his hand. I debate trying to draw my foot away from him, but he's holding it so delicately that I just can't make myself. "I'm going to be a little much, for a little bit."

Oh gods, what the hell does that mean? A little much? "Like freaking out at roller bags?"

He shrugs. "Everything in me says you're the most important thing I've ever been given, and I need to make sure I don't mess it up. Including roller bags. Or pretty much everything else. I don't like things in your space. I don't like things that hurt or inconvenience you. And I'm going to be... obsessive, I guess, about making sure you have everything you need."

There is so much in that statement, a level of intensity I can't hope to match. I squirm a bit, now trying to get my foot back.

He lets me go and looks up at me with those intense brown eyes. "I know you're not prepared for that. I'll do my best to not let it be overwhelming."

I nod, because what else can I do?

He touches my leg again, right above my boot, as if he can't help himself. And then his eyes trail down and get stuck.

It's only then that I realize he can probably see straight up this skirt I have on from that angle.

His hands slowly travel up my calves, fingertips barely a brush on my skin. His eyes are absolutely captivated by whatever he can see up my skirt, and his hands, as if subconsciously, push my legs further open.

I squirm. We're in a crowded airport, there are people everywhere, and I barely know him.

But his eyes feel so good on me, and all I can think about is wanting more.

Suddenly, all thoughts about the ethics of sleeping with someone who wants way more out of it than I do fly out the window. "Bryce?"

"Yes, little witch?" he asks, voice low and raspy, and that sends a bolt of heat through me. I can't help but think of other circumstances where I could get his voice to sound like that.

"Hotel room?"

His eyes leave my legs to find my face, and he nods. "Right. Yes. Of course."
Then, before I can really track what he's doing, he stands up and is extending a
hand to help me up.

I take it and let him wrap an arm around me as we walk.

***

"You liked that," he says, voice somewhere between a whisper and a rumble as we
wait in line for the hotel check-in desk.

I don't need him to clarify what he's talking about, and I don't insult either
of us by pretending I do. I scoff. "What, and you didn't?" Because I saw his eyes,
and he has absolutely no room to throw stones on this front, and if he's going to
try to get a dig in about how easy I am, then he has another thing coming.

"I loved it," he says firmly. "And would like to repeat it as soon as possible."
He looks around furtively. We're not alone, but everyone else in line seems to be
just focused on getting a room for the night, as displaced by the storm as we are.
"You smell so damn good when you like what I'm doing to you."

I gasp, the relief of his reassurance forgotten as soon as he said that. "You can
smell that?"

The grin he gives me is absolutely devastating. "Could probably smell it across
the entire airport. You'll have me trained to find you and drop to my knees within
the week."

Oh fuck. I eye the line in front of us. There better be a room left. Otherwise,
I worry that I'm going to do something stupid.

CHAPTER EIGHTEEN

BRYCE

My little witch is so defensive, like she thinks every word out of my mouth is going to be an attack against her. She thinks I'm insulting her clothes, or insulting her desire, when really, I want to beg for more.

I got her wet by touching her leg and staring up her skirt. I'm desperate to show her what I can actually do with a little of effort. And then, hopefully, she'll really see how much I want her. Need her. How the last thing I'm ever going to do is criticize her for wanting me.

That my mate thinks I'm insulting her all the time is a painful ache inside me. I know I deserve it. I've never been the most pleasant to be around, and now I'm reaping what I sowed.

And I'll do anything to make up for it. To gain her confidence, so she knows that I'm not here to judge her. I'm here to look at her with awe.

"A room, please," I tell the woman at the counter, credit card already out and ready. "A suite, if you have it."

It's not just to show off for Mae, although that's part of it. But I know she's not as ready for this as I am. Giving her her own space might make her more comfortable.

The woman gives me a flat look that tells me she thinks I'm an idiot. "Best I can do is two queens."

Of course. Well, I shouldn't have expected anything else, with all the stranded passengers around. "We'll take it."

Mae waits until we walk away. "How much do I owe you?"

"Nothing."

She has to take long steps to keep up with me, and I slow down even though that only gives her more time to argue with me about money. "Look, I already owe you a lot of money, and—"

"You owe me nothing for this." Like I could take money from her. I'm pretty sure that I wouldn't even be able to take the half a million back from her, even if the spell fails. I'll have to leave it to Celia to work out, as much as I don't want to give her more work, because there's no way I can take back money I know Mae needs for her shop.

Still, I need to put this in a way she'll accept. "I hired you to do a job. Housing you during the job is part of it," I explain.

She opens her mouth to argue more, but doesn't seem to know what to say.

I press my advantage. "Dinner is on me too."

Our room is on the fifth floor, down at the end of the hallway. I let us both in, taking a look around. Half my brain is on checking for security, but the other half is just wishing I took her somewhere more impressive.

Our first night together shouldn't be a mid-range airport hotel with depressingly ugly bedspreads.

"Room service menu is probably on the desk, go start picking out whatever you like," I tell her, already heading into the bathroom.

When I come out, she's sitting on one of the beds, one-page menu in one hand, legs drawn up under her. She's removed her boots and that large overshirt, giving me a truly divine view that makes me stop in my tracks.

I can't believe she thought I was criticizing her clothes earlier. That shirt, painted onto her skin, entirely see through except for the swirls that barely hide her nipples. It will haunt my dreams in the best possible way.

She's a work of art, and I'm going to look at her every chance I get.

She stirs, sliding her feet out from under her. I watch her little feet move, but then she stands from the bed to hand me the menu. "I want the tacos."

"Excellent." I pick up the phone and order, not even glancing at the menu, just copying her order for myself. "It'll be about thirty minutes," I tell her, settling into the desk chair and re-angling it so I can watch her better.

"Great." She falls back onto the bed, sprawling out.

I want to know everything about her. I want to watch her do all these little things. I want her to be making those little wiggling motions against me and not a bed.

She catches me staring. "Do you want to…"

I catch her meaning and shake my head. "Mae, the first time I touch you, we're going to need more than thirty minutes. Believe me."

She stares a moment, mouth falling open, but then she pulls herself together and smirks. Doesn't matter. I can still smell that I turned her on. She's thinking about it, what that first time will be like.

"You have a high opinion of yourself." She pauses, as if she's considering it, and something in me puffs with pride, that she's clearly thinking of why I might hold that opinion. "Well, you've had a thousand years to practice."

"Mhm." I'm not going to apologize for it. "And I fully plan on letting you benefit from all that practice."

She's thinking about it again. I can smell it. Good.

But I have to change the subject, or I really am going to simply fall to my knees in front of her every time I smell her arousal. And that won't work, because I definitely plan on taking my time with her. Tonight, if she'll let me.

"You said you wanted to travel?" I ask, desperate for a change of topic. "What do you want to see?"

She falls back against the bed entirely again, head on a pillow and body starfished to take up as much space as possible. She looks at the ceiling instead of at me. "Where don't I want to go? I used to read atlases, you know."

I think of her as a child, sixty years ago, in some New York City apartment, reading atlases under the covers. Maybe using her magic to light the space.

"But you never traveled?"

She exhales slowly. "Costs money," she admits. "And I never had much. I was saving. And I was close, too, but…"

"But?"

"The shop."

She says it with absolutely no warmth in her voice, like the shop is some sort of soul-sucking creature.

"You don't sound happy about that." She'd agreed to do a spell she wasn't even sure she could do, put herself through what looks like a lot of suffering, to look after her store. I lean forward, waiting for her explanation.

"You know the shop was Greta's. She's my cousin. I didn't ask for this. Never wanted it."

"So how'd you end up with it?"

"Greta left. Got married. She's totally out of contact. Some eternal honeymoon. And I got stuck with her shop."

And she says she was close to being able to travel. The picture takes shape in my mind, showing me the massive burden dumped on her. "No one else to take it?"

She goes still, like I've hit on something she doesn't want to talk about. "No one Greta or I would want to have that place. So, whatever. I look out for it. Keep the doors open. It's—well, hey. I'm only sixty. Plenty of time to travel later," she says, voice full of false cheer. She sits up in bed so she can watch me, crossing her legs under her. "Tell me about you."

"What about me?" I'll tell her anything she wants to know.

She stops for a minute, thinking, and tilts her head. "I don't know. I'm going to be honest with you, I'm trying to figure out what I can ask without leading you on."

"Leading me on?"

"You clearly want things out of this. And I... look, you hired me to do a job. Are you absolutely someone I'd fuck? Yeah. But this eternal mates thing, like I said earlier, it's way, way out of left field here. And I don't want to make you think I'm ready for that when I'm not."

I take a deep breath. Celia and Heath had it so easy, with mates that just understood.

Not that I'd trade Mae for anything. Just the thought of my mate being someone who's not her fills me with a cold, spreading dread.

"Tell me anything you want. Ask me anything you want. And I won't read into it past what you tell me to," I promise her. Not exactly a lie. I won't take our relationship past whatever she's comfortable with. She'll set all the terms.

But will I think about it? Absolutely.

"How's it feel?" she blurts out, and I can tell from the way she bites her lip after that she did not mean to ask it out loud. But she said it, and I'm more than happy to tell her.

"It feels like the world makes sense. Like I look at you and the world suddenly has light in it."

She looks down at herself, at her all-black outfit. "Light?"

"Trust me. You could never be anything but light."

She bites her lip again, thinking, and I wait for her. "You realize how crazy this feels to me? It's like everything changed. You didn't even really like me, and now—"

"I liked you plenty," I interrupt, because I cannot let her go on thinking that. "Trust me. I know I didn't show it. I'm not exactly friendly and I was working and I never fuck around on the job. I take it very seriously." I shake my head, wanting to reach for her but restraining myself. "Honestly, if you had any idea how much time I spent thinking about you, and worried about how much I was thinking about you." Even at the full moon, I'd been thinking of her.

Looking back, there were plenty of signs. The fact that others no longer interested me in the slightest, the way she consumed my dreams and haunted me during the moon, the way all my normal pack instincts were overridden... I should have known.

"But that's it! You take your job seriously. I can fully accept that every moment since we met, I was a liability to your job. You needed Greta and got stuck with me, then I fucked up the spell and already spent some of your money. You should have been a hardass to me, that makes sense and I expect it. And now you're telling me you like looking up my skirt and want to, what, start a life together? Forgive all my transgressions against you?"

Not exactly how I'd categorize it, but it's not wrong, because yes, I loved looking up her skirt and I'd very much like to start a life together. "The only thing that would ever win out over my duty to the pack is my mate. Every wolf knows that. So now things make sense, why I was willing to give you the second chance, why I couldn't make myself believe you would screw us over."

"I wasn't, you know," she says, voice quiet, almost meek in a way I instinctively hate. "I wasn't trying to screw you over. I swear I wasn't."

"I know. I trust you."

"You definitely should not, based on what you just said."

I can't help it. I can't do anything else but trust her. But I don't think she'd like that argument. In her own way, I think she's actually trying to protect me, which is sweet. Unnecessary, but sweet.

"Fate wouldn't pair me with a person who would hurt the pack. I have every confidence in you, Mae," I tell her.

"You wolves are stubborn, aren't you?"

"You have no idea."

She huffs. "Fine, then. Just be forewarned—I'm not convinced."

"You don't have to be." Yet. I can take this slow, take my time to convince her I'll be a good mate for her.

CHAPTER NINETEEN

MAE

Dinner is some pretty mediocre tacos, but the meal is much improved by Bryce describing the village I'm going to see tomorrow.

My first non-New York destination, assuming this airport doesn't count. And it sounds like a legitimate fairy tale.

A valley so far removed from humans, surrounded by forests and mountains, beautiful and remote and full of all the natural beauty I can only imagine.

I really, really hope I can do that spell. It sounds like an amazing place, and I'd hate to leave on a bad note.

He inhales his tacos, even when he's doing most of the talking, but he waits patiently for me to finish mine after. Then, he sets the tray and the plates in the hallway, double-checking the door lock when he comes back in.

It's like the whole atmosphere changes, like the air takes on a charge. I've felt spells do this to a space, giving off an almost electric feeling, but I don't think I've ever just felt it naturally with another person.

I decide I can't blame myself as I look him over.

Bryce Crae is the type of guy that people drool over. Ridiculously tall and built in a way that just has to be supernatural, Bryce's deep tan and now tousled dark hair just completes the look of tall, dark, and handsome. When paired with the intensity of his golden brown eyes, people probably melt for him.

I certainly am. I squeeze my thighs together, looking at him and not even being subtle about it.

He looks too big, standing there in this little hotel room. No one would ever have trouble believing he's a thousand year old werewolf, honestly. He just carries an energy too big and too grand for mundane spaces like this.

And then there's me, forgettable, mediocre, and has to dress like I do just so people don't entirely miss me in the crowd.

Except for when he looks at me like this, because I don't feel forgettable now. No, I suddenly feel more powerful than any spell has ever made me feel. I feel like I could light the world on fire.

I don't tell him that, don't give him any more support for his eternal mates thing. But I let my thighs fall open on the bed, slowly, invitingly, giving him a perfect view up my skirt again.

His eyes go heavy and he takes what seems to be an unconscious step forward. "Mae," he says, voice somehow impossibly lower. "I need you to tell me what you're up for tonight."

I swallow and look him over, but I already know my answer. "I want you tonight, Bryce. No expectations, just fuck me. Please."

I thought that answer might disappoint him, but I get just the opposite. No, I get the gigantically tall werewolf prowling to the bed I'm on, then letting his knees hit the edge, going to his hands and knees to crawl over me, caging me in.

I bite my lip, looking at the delicious wall of muscle surrounding me. "I should mention that I'm not, like, passive in bed or anything," I say absently, already reaching out to trace his chest over his shirt. I don't know much about werewolves, but I hear they can get pretty aggressive in bed. Which is all well and good, but he should know I bite back.

He immediately sits back on his knees to pull his shirt off over his head, throwing it somewhere on the floor behind him. "Good," he says. "I want you very, very involved."

He moves back over me, leaving his chest and abs on display for me, and I waste no time touching them, trailing one finger over his stomach, watching the muscles twitch under my touch.

One of his hands moves to cup my thigh, playing with the gap in the fishnet tights. "I have been staring at these all day," he rasps.

I look down at my thick thighs in disbelief. "Seriously?"

His hand suddenly leaves my thigh to move to my face, pinching my chin and turning my face up to meet his eyes. "Want them wrapped around my head," he says, voice deadly serious.

Fuck.

He is not fucking around, and this man might be the death of me. I press my thighs together.

A delighted smile breaks over his face. "You like that."

"You ever met someone who didn't?" I shoot back.

He tilts my chin a little further and leans in to kiss me, deep and insistent. I grab onto his head, lacing my fingers in his hair to hold him to me, dragging him closer.

He bites at my bottom lip, then soothes it with his tongue before pulling away. "We're not talking about someone else," he says gently, and it takes me a minute to even remember the quip I made before he kissed me. Gods, my brain is scrambled.

I tighten my grip on his hair, pulling him in for another kiss. "Got—got it," I promise between kisses.

He breaks the kiss to press kisses along my jaw. "Just us tonight. And I'm going to learn exactly what you like."

I'm sure I have a comment. I'm sure I do. But I completely forget it as he sucks on my neck, and all I can do is moan.

He lets go of my face and puts his hand back on my thigh, trailing his hand higher and higher between kisses.

I let my thighs fall further and further open until they're completely constricted by the skirt and I have to choose between taking it off and rucking it up around my hips.

I reach for the button at my waist, wiggling under him so I can unbutton the skirt and then push it down my thighs. Bryce catches on quickly, helping me pull it down until he's kneeling at my feet, throwing the skirt behind him and looking me over with hungry eyes. "Fuck, Mae."

He looks at me with such sincerity that I decide right then and there to give into it. That I can let everything else go. Sure, Bryce is really, really into me. He wants to fuck me enough that just the look in his eyes makes me wet. I can accept that, as long as I don't think about the consequences further down the line.

I look down at where his cock is tenting his jeans. Not thinking about consequences? Easy.

"C'mere," I say, crooking a finger as if to pull him up the bed, and he falls forward like I really did pull him.

He kisses my neck again, but then moves down to my collarbones, my chest, and finally to the edge of the bodysuit, pulling it slightly to get to the skin underneath but being oddly careful not to stretch it out.

One hand comes up to cup my left tit, squeezing it before he finds my nipple through the material, pinching lightly until my back bows off the bed, seeking more stimulation.

He chuckles darkly and moves so he can lick the other nipple through the material. I grab at his hair, not sure if I want to tug him off or hold him closer.

"That's it, beautiful," he murmurs, his breath a puff of hot air that makes me shiver. "I got you."

I bet he does. I bet he could make me come without much additional effort. And I could argue that it's just been a while, that pretty much anyone could make me come, but I know that'd be a lie. His every move is confident, assured. He knows what he's doing. He's already identified ways to make me weak at the knees.

I want to shake that assurance. Just a little bit.

I move my hands from his hair to his shoulders, then to his chest, shoving at him. I know I don't really have a hope of moving him, but as I expected, he moves willingly, sitting up immediately, brow furrowed, like he thinks something is wrong. But the expression melts into one of absolute lust as I keep pushing, guiding him onto his back. His eyes are burning hot and don't leave my face as I move him exactly where I want him.

He goes easily enough, and I swing my stocking-clad legs over him to straddle his stomach. "My turn," I tell him.

He makes a show of laying his hands on the blankets by his head. "I'm at your mercy, Mae."

Yeah, as if. Still, even knowing it can never really be true—not without some enchanted ropes or cuffs, maybe—a shot of warm power fills my core anyway.

I rock myself against his stomach experimentally, trying to find an angle that will tease my clit. I can't really get the angle, but it's worth it anyway, watching his face tighten as he watches me move. "Little further back, darling," he says through gritted teeth.

I reach behind me and palm his cock through his jeans, and he bucks under me. I smile. "Like that?" Just to make it sink in, I rock on his abs again and squeeze his cock at the same time.

He groans, but his eyes are fully focused on my face. "If you let me, I swear I can make you feel better than that," he says.

I just bet he could. "Hm, not yet," I say instead, rocking again, just to watch his face.

He doesn't disappoint, watching me right back, and his gaze makes my skin prickle, like it's a touch all of its own.

Apparently, I've pushed him past the point of his keeping his hands to himself phase, because both hands come up to cup my tits, hefting them in his huge hands. "I fucking love this shirt," he rumbles, squeezing. "Now, how the fuck do I get it off you?"

I laugh; I can't help it. "That would require me to get off you," I tease.

He growls and squeezes my tits again, then surges upright, with me perched in his lap. "Fine then. Be quick."

I get off his lap and off the bed, pulling off the fishnets and discarding them on the floor before I unsnap the body suit and turn back around to him. "You should take your pants off—" I start to say, but then I watch as he just gapes at me.

"Come here," he murmurs, sliding so he's seated on the edge of the bed.

I walk between his spread legs. "Take your pants off for me, Bryce," I say as firmly as I can manage.

He huffs. "Give a man a minute to appreciate a work of art," he mumbles, and then pushes the straps off my shoulders before pushing the bodysuit to the floor.

I want to snap back, want to push away the work of art comment. But I don't. I can't. Not when I can still feel the heat of his gaze, not when he flutters his fingertips, feather light, over my skin.

He starts on my hips, a gentle exploration of the skin there, pressing soothing touches into the lines where the bodysuit and the waistband of the fishnets cut into my skin. Then he moves up across my body, his touch reverent and slow. Just when I'm starting to squirm, just when this is verging uncomfortably into the territory of things I definitely don't want to think about tonight, he finds my tits again.

"Fucking stunning," he murmurs, tracing maddeningly feather-light circles, getting closer and closer to my nipple with each pass. Finally, finally, he reaches my nipple and pinches, making me let out an embarrassingly loud moan and push myself into his hands.

He takes a deep, obvious inhale. "Do you have any idea how good you smell right now?"

"Take off your pants," I force myself to say. "And get inside me."

Chapter Twenty

Bryce

I could never resist such a beautiful invitation. Not from her.

I force myself to let go of her tits—and that'll have to be remedied later, I'll need to spend hours holding them, licking them, sucking them, showing her how spell-bound I am by them—and hastily undo my pants, raising my hips enough to shove them down.

She steps back so I can get them off, and I growl in protest, but really all her stepping back does is draw my eyes like a magnet to her cunt.

I've been smelling her for hours. Been acclimatizing myself to her scent, been fucking reveling in every drop I get. And now I see her, wet curls dark and glistening, protected by her soft thighs.

She takes another teasing step back at my growl, but all it does is part her thighs just slightly, giving me another tease of what lies between them.

If she hadn't already said the words *get inside me*, I'd go to my knees for her right here and now. But I can't deny her request, so I gesture her closer. "Come here. Let me get you ready."

She doesn't move, staring at my cock. "Gods, you're huge."

I reach down to stroke myself, slowly, watching her eyes track my movement. There's a little of trepidation in her eyes, yes, but I can still smell how much she wants this.

"I'll take care of you," I promise her. My voice is low and rough, barely more than a growl with my need for her. "Come here, Mae. I promise I'll take care of you."

She steps closer, her body sensuous, every curve on perfect display as she walks.

Gods, I'm the luckiest wolf in the world. To have this, her, forever.

I know she doesn't feel the bond, and she's not sold on forever yet. I don't think a really good orgasm will necessarily change her mind.

But it can't hurt.

I grab her hips as soon as she's close enough and tug her until she's straddling my lap, kneeling over me. I spread my thighs just a little wider, forcing her to spread her own thighs, giving me a mouth-watering view of her cunt.

I don't waste any time, reaching down to stroke over her clit. She yelps and bucks her hips in surprise, grabbing at my shoulders for balance.

The move puts her tits right at my eye level, and I don't waste the opportunity, sucking her nipple into my mouth just as I circle her clit again.

The moan she lets out is long and low and delicious. I want to hear it every night for the rest of our lives. Will consider the day wasted if I don't.

"That's it, beautiful," I murmur, pulling back enough to breathe on her now-moist nipple. Her thighs try to tighten around my hand, but she can't move them, not with my own thighs between her knees.

I rock one finger into her, pressing the heel of my hand against her clit, and she lets out a gasp. "Oh, oh, Bryce, I—"

"That's it," I murmur again. I slide my finger in and out of her slowly, encouraging her to start a rhythm of her own rocking against my hand.

When she rocked against my stomach earlier, I could see she couldn't quite get the angle she wanted. I think it's safe to say I found it here as she rocks and moans, her nails biting into my shoulders. I slide a second finger in, then a third, watching her rock against my palm, making sure I find that place inside of her with every pass of my fingers, making her gasp.

"You ready for me?" I ask her. She's moaning and rocking entirely without my prompting, chasing her own pleasure, and it's so fucking beautiful to watch.

"Mh—mhm," she gasps, nodding quickly. "Ready."

I lean forward to nip at her breast again. "Come on my hand first," I say, pressed into her skin. "Soak my hand for me, little witch. Then I'll fuck you like you want." I'm demanding and I know it, but I need to see her fall apart and am greedy for it now.

She moans again, then rocks faster against my hand, chasing that high. When her cunt contracts around my fingers, she loses all sense of her rhythm, almost collapsing onto me, and I take over, coaxing her through her orgasm.

I use my free hand to wrap around her back, supporting her as she moans softly, coming down from that high. I carefully extract my other hand from between her thighs. "Beautiful, Mae," I murmur into her hair. "That was fucking perfect."

I take the hand covered in her come and raise it to my mouth, licking every inch of it clean. And I watch her watch me while I do it.

Her eyes are heavy lidded and her mouth parted slightly. Her tongue darts out to wet that plump bottom lip.

"Want a taste?" I ask her.

She blinks at me, maybe not ready to speak yet. That's okay.

My hand is already clean, so I reach down between us again, drawing my fingers through her folds, careful to avoid her clit for the moment, to give her a minute to come down from one orgasm before I push her for another. Then, I offer my hand to her.

She doesn't move for a second. "You're fucking delicious, Mae," I tell her.

She leans forward and sucks my index finger into her mouth, licking it clean, apparently leaving the rest for me, which is a delicacy I'll more than happily accept. But as she's sucking my finger, giving me filthy thoughts, she reaches down and grips my cock.

"In me," she says firmly, pulling back from my finger.

"Whatever the lady wants," I say, and think through options. What's the best way to fuck her tonight? How can I make sure I make this really fucking good for her?

But like she told me, she isn't passive in bed, and she's already climbing off my lap and crawling further up the bed, getting on her hands and knees and wiggling her ass at me.

My mouth goes dry. What a glorious, perfect fucking ass. Before I know what I'm doing, I've clamped my hands on her hips and leaned down to bite at her ass.

"Seriously?" she demands, but I can smell her getting even wetter.

"Seriously," I say, pulling back and admiring the teeth marks I just left behind. "You seriously have a perfect ass and I'm never going to be able to resist it."

She snorts. "It's just fat, Bryce."

"It's fucking glorious and if I didn't think you'd kill me, I'd spend a few hours proving it to you. But," I continue, reaching between her thighs to stroke along her folds, rubbing briefly over her clit before moving on, "I know where you want me."

I don't waste any more time. I line my cock up, feeding it into her slowly, waiting to see if she tenses up, if she needs me to stop. But she just groans and pushes back against me, trying to get more.

"Greedy," I murmur. "Let me set the pace for a minute, hm?" I know I'm big, as she's already pointed out. I don't want to hurt her.

"I... like... the... stretch," she grunts, still trying to push back for more.

"Do you?" I ask, feeling the grin form. Because I can smell it, smell her wetness, smell how she's dripping all over my cock. She's telling the truth.

And she wants this. Wants me.

I rock into her fully until I'm seated deep within her. She moans at that, then twists her hips, trying to get me exactly where she wants me.

Good. I rock with her until we find that place, where she starts absolutely dripping all over me and her arms go out from under her, falling to her elbows and moaning loud enough that I might consider worrying about thin hotel room walls.

"That's it, beautiful," I murmur. "Let me give you what you want." I already know I'm not going to last much longer, that Mae is literally a fantasy made flesh in so many ways. She's beautiful. I've been dreaming about her, teasing myself with thoughts of her every night. And I've longed for my mate for centuries.

I need to make sure she comes before I do. I need to make this good for her.

I rock into her, slow and deep, dragging myself over the spot inside her that makes her whine every time I do it. With one hand, I trace up her spine, back down to her hips, and back again. And with my other hand, I slide it around her, finding her clit and beginning to tease it, pushing her closer and closer to the edge.

"Bryce, I, I... oh, gods!" She's practically shouting now. To know I make her feel like this, that I can give this to her, is quite possibly the greatest accomplishment of my life.

When she comes, she shouts my name loud enough that I'm sure the neighbors hear it. Her cunt clenches around me, and I can't resist it, not her tight heat, not her sweet scent, not her beautiful noises, and I follow her over the edge, gasping her name as I do.

It takes me a long moment to make myself pull out of her, to lose that tight warm heat. But eventually I make myself pull out and gently roll her so she's on her back when she starts to collapse completely forward.

She's now sprawled on the bed, a flush on her face and chest, her thighs still spread to show off the absolute treasure that lies between them. Her eyes are drooping closed, and I want to make sure she's comfortable before I let her fall asleep.

I get a washcloth to wipe us both down, making sure I'm as gentle as I can be while I clean her up. Then I shut off the lights and crawl into the bed beside her, holding my breath.

There are two beds in this room, and I wait for her to kick me out, to tell me to go get my own. Or, hell, for her to leave me here and go to the bed that we didn't just come all over.

But it doesn't happen. So, hesitantly, I reach out and haul her closer to me with a hand on her ass, pulling her into my arms.

"You okay?" I ask, needing to check, needing to know what she's thinking.

She smiles at me. It's a tired smile, but it is a smile and it makes my heart clench. "You are really good at that," she admits.

I laugh lightly, kissing her cheek. "At your service."

Seriously, I want to tell her. Whenever, wherever she wants. I am fully one hundred percent at her service when it comes to this type of thing. I am more than happy to let her push me into whatever positions she wants at any time.

But before I can say any of that, her eyes have started to drift closed, so I just kiss her forehead, hold her closer, and let her sweet scent help me drift off to sleep.

CHAPTER TWENTY-ONE

BRYCE

I wake up in the morning with a witch entirely on top of me, with her hair tickling my nose, and with my cock as hard as stone.

The hard cock isn't anything new. The witch has had me hard every single time I've woken up since the day we met.

What is new is being so surrounded by her. By her physically, yes, but also by her scent. I realize only now that's what was missing from the dreams. I could never scent her.

Now I take a deep, deep inhale of her hair. Fucking perfect.

I look at the clock on the bedside table and curse. We only have an hour and a half until our flight boards, and I need to choose between licking her cunt until she screams and feeding her breakfast.

Just when I'm about to decide fuck it, we can eat on the plane, she stirs in my arms.

"Good morning."

She huffs, half rolling off of me, and I feel the loss like a blow. "Not a morning person," she admits after a moment of staring at the ceiling. "I need coffee."

Coffee. Right. I look around the hotel room, but don't see a coffee maker. "We'll have to get it in the airport," I say apologetically.

She nods, slowly, as if it takes her a long minute to process that. "I'm going to be very useless until I get it," she warns me, swinging her legs over the side of the bed so she can get up.

Naked, beautiful ass on display, and it takes an act of strength I didn't know I was capable of to not dive forward to catch her by the hips and drag that ass back to me.

My mate wants coffee. That, I can provide for her.

***

It takes her almost thirty minutes to get ready for the day. I'd say something, but all the breath leaves my body the minute I see her clothes.

"Is everything you own like this?" I ask her, eyeing the shirt that's entirely see-through except for the black lace bra underneath.

"Like what?" she asks, and I hear the tension creeping into her voice as she turns to the mirror to do something with her hair.

"Liable to make me come in my pants."

She stops, hands held in midair, and smiles at me, and I think that one smile is warmer than anything else I've seen from her so far. "You're easy to please."

I really, really am not. Except, when it comes to her beautiful body, teasing me like this? Apparently, I am.

She finally deems herself ready to leave, so I take her bag and we make our way back into the chaos of the airport, heading straight to the nearest coffee shop.

She sucks down the coffee like it's her last meal, then looks disappointed at the cup.

"What's wrong?" I ask, sipping my own coffee much slower.

"Coffee doesn't quite do it anymore," she mumbles. "I usually dump in a stimulant spell, but they're liquid and I didn't want to explain them to the TSA, so I left them behind. And I'll need like an hour to make more."

"Stimulant spells?"

"Think mystical, concentrated caffeine."

Sounds like a health hazard, but I don't say it. That seems like a battle to fight another time.

"So that's the type of magic you do?"

She shrugs. "I've always preferred the immediately practical stuff, you know? The small things. I don't want to do grand-scale things. I like my magic to be just for me. The little things that make my life easier."

I nod and look her over. "Like enchanting your clothes to keep you warm." I let my eyes linger, hoping it finally helps her understand I am fully on board for how she dresses.

It seems the message gets through, because she flushes and ducks her head to her empty cup, and the scent that I'm already well-trained to come running for permeates the air.

Excellent.

I check my watch and see that we still have thirty minutes before we need to board. I look at the rest of my coffee, but who needs coffee when I could have something much sweeter? "Drink this," I say, handing her the cup, which she takes immediately, greedily. "And follow me."

She doesn't ask any questions, just sips the coffee, following me as I look around the airport, and—there.

She stops. "That is not the gate."

"Good observation," I mutter, using one hand on the small of her back to steer her towards the single-stall family restroom, yanking the door open with more force than necessary. I usher her inside, then close and lock the door behind us. I take the now-empty coffee cup from her hand and throw it away, then prowl towards her.

"Are you serious?" she demands, looking around the small space.

We're hardly the first people to fuck in public restrooms. We're probably not the first people to fuck in this particular public restroom either, but somehow I don't think that argument will convince her. "I am so, so serious, little witch," I tell her, stepping closer, closing the distance between us in two strides so I can work a hand into her hair to pull her close for a kiss, tilting her head up as I bend down to her. I pull away after a moment, trailing my mouth along her jaw. "I am so serious that I don't want to wait any longer to make you feel good."

I move her so she's against the wall, backing her up slowly, watching her eyes go heavy-lidded as we move. She wants this, is thinking about it, is getting wet over it—

Gods, I want to taste that.

Once I have her against the wall, I attempt to drop to my knees, but she stops me, her hands gripping my shoulders to try to tug me back upright. "What are you doing?"

"What does it look like I'm doing?" I ask, because I thought it was more than a little obvious.

"You are not eating me out in a public bathroom."

Okay, fine. I can work with that.

"You just let me know when we get to a place where I can eat you out, then," I tell her, my voice getting raspy as I think about it.

"You really want to?" she asks, as if she's surprised.

"I—want—to," I promise, voice little more than a rumble as I think about it. Understatement of the century, really.

Her mouth has fallen open slightly. Maybe she didn't believe me last time.

"I—okay, then. Not here!" she says hurriedly, as if worried I'll pounce on her. "Some other time."

"Some other time," I echo, then move my hands to slide under her shirt, teasing the waistband of those skin-tight pants. "Can I do something else to make you come right now, though? I can smell you, Mae, and I want to make you come."

She bites her lip, and I make a mental note of that image, to save it for the rest of my life. "Your fingers?" she asks, and then she looks down. "Last night, you were—I was—"

Last night she rode my hand and made herself come and it was so beautiful that I will remember it for the rest of my damn life, even if I live thousands of years more. I will absolutely finger her whenever she asks me to.

"I would love for you to soak my fingers," I tell her, already reaching for the button on the pants.

I open them and stare at the underwear underneath, absolutely see-through. "Gods, you're gorgeous," I murmur, and she ducks her head again.

I'll tell her as often as possible. To remind her every day, every hour, that she's perfect.

As I get to know her better, I'll just have more things to praise her for. For now, I'll have to start with her being smart and funny and so damn beautiful that it takes my breath away.

I push the panties to the side and slide my finger over her folds, drawing it through her wetness a few times before I drag it over her clit. She gasps, a high, breathy thing, as if she's trying to suppress it but can't entirely stop herself.

Good. That's exactly how it should feel when we're together.

I want to drag this out, but I know we don't have long before our flight, and I have a vested interest in getting her home. So I push my finger inside of her, waiting until I hear that breathy moan again before adding a second, and using my thumb to tease her clit while she gasps and rocks against my hand.

"That's it," I murmur, watching with rapt attention as her eyes fall closed, as she bites her lower lip to keep her sounds in. "That's it, little witch. Let me make you come. Let me make you feel good."

She nods, seemingly half-hearing what I'm saying, and I crook my fingers inside her, searching for just the spot until she loses control and moans my name.

She puts a hand over her mouth, and just in time, too, because I hear the moan she's trying to keep back as her cunt squeezes my fingers and her thighs start to shake. Her orgasm absolutely soaks my hand, and I tease her for a minute longer until she uses her free hand to still my wrist.

"Enough," she says, trying to sound firm, but her voice shakes. I nod and use my clean hand to steady her by grabbing her hip.

"And you?" she asks.

I look at my watch and shrug. "Oh, I got everything I want," I tell her, making eye contact as I raise my hand to my mouth and carefully, completely, lick my fingers clean.

Not entirely true. There are definitely other things I want. But her taste on my tongue? It's practically perfect, and I wouldn't trade it for anything.

Chapter Twenty-Two

Mae

We barely make it to the gate. Our boarding group has already long-since been called, so we get in line with the last passengers and get onboard.

When we're on the plane, Bryce once again gives me the window even though my ticket is marked as the middle seat. Once he shoves my bag in the overhead compartment, he slides in next to me and immediately pushes up the armrest so he can wrap his arm around me and tug me into his side.

I go willingly. More than willingly, truth be told. Everything about him is comfortable. Incredibly comfortable, in a way I'd never expect. Because here is this physically fit, thousand-year-old werewolf who clearly has some level of power in his pack. And he doesn't judge my life, or me, or my looks, or how I dress. Every time I expect him to zig, he zags, in the best way possible.

Like the way he watches me, attention entirely on me, eyes dark with an intensity that makes me shiver. The way he touches me, almost reverent.

The way he talks about wanting to eat me out.

I suppress a shiver. All this is bordering on things I don't want to think about. Things I'm not allowed to think about. All of it is too close to considering this as some part of my big picture, when it just can't be.

I am here to do a job, I remind myself. A job I was hired to do and already fucked up once. And once that job is done, I need to go home, no matter how good the sex is in the meantime. I need to go home and take care of the shop and find a way to tell Violet that I probably can't afford to keep them on. I need to go back to my life, and that life doesn't feature sexy werewolves.

He has his own job, his own life, I remind myself. We're just not meant to be.

And anyway, meant to be? That's long-term talk. That's we've-been-dating-a-while talk, not we-fucked-for-the-first-time-last-night. And if it's not, then I'm buying into his fated mates thing, and I just can't do that.

Because I can't be fated for him. That's absolutely entirely impossible. Just look at us.

Well. Look at him. Looking like that in the seat next to me, huge and powerful, with those serious eyes turned to me. He's spread his thighs slightly, trying to get comfortable, and I can't help but watch them flex. Gods, he's built. Like, I bet he can pick me up and carry me around with ease.

I want him to, biting my lip just thinking about it. That would be hot. To have him pick me up and fuck me, using nothing but his own strength to hold me up.

I realize too late that he knows what I'm thinking. He might not be a mind-reader and might not know the details, but, as he keeps reminding me, he can smell it when my thoughts get dirtier.

I watch him shift in his seat again, his eyes rapt on me. I lay a hand on his upper thigh, dangerously close to his cock. "Regret not making time for your turn?" I ask him.

"If there was only time for one of us, it's always going to be you," he says, then licks his lips in an obvious indication of what he means.

Gods, yeah. Okay. Whether this is bordering on leading him on, regardless of our fundamental difference of opinion on what our relationship will be, I can't ignore this. I'll physically combust if I try to ignore him while we're in his village.

I'll be there for however long it takes to do the spell and confirm it. And in that time, I'll let this play out. Let him lick me to his heart's content, get him to fuck me against a wall or something. Let every dirty fantasy we can come up with take over in every free moment we have.

And afterwards, I'll walk away. I'll have to, and he can't pretend he's surprised. I've never lied to him about what I want.

He tightens his arm around me, and I lean further into his side, burying my face in his chest. He smells good. Something a little spicy.

The scent helps lull me to sleep.

***

The landing is thankfully smoother this time, and I'm ready to admit that planes aren't terrible. Bryce texts someone as we wait to get off the plane, then grabs my bag and walks behind me as we exit.

He guides us to the pickup area, where a big black SUV, the kind that I usually see driving celebrities around, is waiting.

He opens the back door and nods for me to enter. I scoot across as he follows me. "Jake, this is Mae. Mae, Jake."

Jake turns and gives me a half smile. "Nice to meet you and have you with us." He seems sincere enough, so I wonder how much Bryce has told him. Maybe he doesn't know about the spell fuck up. Or maybe Bryce told him the mate thing, and the guy is just excited about that.

Either way, he turns his full attention to Bryce. "Your sister is looking for you."

Bryce goes unexpectedly tense at that. "Well, guess we better not keep her waiting."

He doesn't seem inclined to explain that, but that's okay. His sister really isn't my business. It's not like I'm going to be a part of the family.

Instead, I watch out the window, taking in my new surroundings. As we get further away from the airport, the buildings thin out until they're few and far between, trees and rolling hills taking over the landscape.

"It's beautiful," I whisper to myself, thinking of those rolling hills, those trees. I bet they look good covered in snow in the winter. Unlike New York, which just turns into a gray and brown mess.

Bryce places his hand on my back, the heat of his huge palm seeping into my skin. He doesn't say anything, though, and doesn't interrupt my watching. He just rubs slightly, his hand making soothing motions as I watch a new world pass the window.

***

When we reach the village—exactly as beautiful as Bryce's descriptions promised—Jake drives us to a big, stately looking house closer to the opening of the valley than the town itself.

"Here we are. Celia's place," he explains, looking at me.

Celia. Why is that name ringing a bell? I don't think Bryce named his siblings when he talked briefly about them.

There's a ton of Celia's in the world; I'm sure whatever I remember has absolutely nothing to do with this. Maybe someone I went to school with, or worked with.

"C'mon," Bryce mumbles. "Don't want to keep her waiting."

Like she was summoned, a tall, willowy blonde opens the door. I try to see the resemblance to Bryce, but I get nothing.

"You're late," she calls.

"Bethany. I texted."

Bethany?

She smiles. "Yeah, well. I cooked yesterday, so you're going to have to deal with leftovers."

"I can live with that," Bryce says, and he puts his hand on my back again. "My sister's mate," he mumbles to me, gently nudging me towards the door. "Before we eat, where's Celia?"

"Also eating," a voice calls from inside. "Hurry it up, Bryce."

Bethany steps inside to let us into the house, showing us into a comfortable-looking home, probably ten times bigger than Greta's apartment. There's a living room with multiple comfortable sofas, and beyond that, a long dining table, currently almost full.

"I didn't realize everyone would be here," Bryce says, his hand stiffening on my back.

"What, you bring your mate home and don't expect all of us?" a man says. He looks just like Bryce, the only significant difference being a large scar through one eye.

Family, then. Family that Bryce has already told the whole mate thing to, and are now here to ask questions and expect things of me I am not down for and—

Bethany re-enters the room, smiling softly. "Heath, introduce yourself like someone with manners."

Heath gives me an apologetic smile. "Heath, obviously. This is Chase," he says, gesturing to the man sitting next to him with small horns half-hidden by his hair. "Callum—" another wolf who looks similar to Bryce, just with longer hair—"You've met Bethany, and this is Celia."

Celia looks like her brothers, well built and dark, and her attention is currently almost entirely focused on her plate. Bethany makes her way to the seat next to Celia and puts her hand on top of hers, and Celia looks up. "So. You're here to fix the border spell?"

My mouth goes dry. How much did Bryce tell these people? "I—yeah, I am."

She nods. "Good. Let's talk terms." She pushes back from the table and stares at everyone else around the table. "If one of you so much as breathes on this stew, I will kick your ass. Bethany made it especially for me and if any of it's missing, I'll know."

"I made more," Bethany says, shaking her head but smiling.

"And you made this portion for me, so it'll be here when I get back. C'mon," she says, directing the last part at Bryce and I. "Business first, then food."

Celia leads us into a nice office at the other end of the house, where she sits behind a large desk and gestures for us to take the chairs on the other side.

I'm starting to get the feeling that I've missed something here.

Celia leans forward, hands steepled together. "First off: I'm so glad my brother found his mate. And I'm glad you agreed to come help with this spell. But I'm sure you understand that, as leader of this pack, I can't take whoops as a reason to give you a second chance, even if you're Bryce's mate." Her eyes flick to her brother. "Especially if you're his mate. He's going to be too quick to believe anything you say."

"Celia," Bryce growls.

My mind is spinning. As leader of this pack? Celia is…

I remember where I heard her name now. Bryce told me multiple times that he was working on behalf of Queen Celia.

He just never mentioned that she is his damn sister. And that makes him… what? A prince?

Just chalk up another one in the reasons we'll never work column.

I force myself to pull it together. This is about the job, and I have to do the job. And finally, someone is questioning the failure. She isn't wrong; Bryce has been way too trusting, considering I have half a million dollars sitting in my business account and gave them nothing to show for it.

"I said I'd do the spell because I assumed my cousin had left it behind in a spell book," I tell her. "I asked for two days to find it. When I told Bryce it was done, I genuinely believed I'd done it correctly. I didn't realize until he showed back up that the person I trusted to help me translate it lied to me."

"And you have an accurate translation now?" she asks, voice even. She doesn't sound like she's against me, which is a relief. Everything about her bearing is neutral, like she really does just want to hear my side of the story.

"No. Not unless you know ancient Sumerian?" I ask.

"Can't say I do."

"Then I'm using some notes Greta left behind and some spell casting techniques I know to do it a different way." I take a deep breath. "If it doesn't work, I swear I'll give you the money back. I don't really know another witch to point you at, but I'm sure you can find someone. And if you do find someone who can translate the spell, I'll hand it over."

There. That's a lot to give. Witches don't hand over their spells. I'm not sure if they know that or not, but I do, and it feels like a fair concession.

As for the money, I have no idea how I'll pay that back. Most of it is still in the business account, but a non-zero amount has already been spent. I'll have to see if they'll do some sort of payment plan.

The shop won't be able to stay open if I have to give the money back. It's that simple. I'll have failed Greta's one and only ask of me my entire life.

I don't say any of that out loud, of course. That's my problem. Queen Celia's problem is just if she trusts me enough to let me try the spell.

She looks at me for a long, long moment, and I feel Bryce getting more and more tense beside me. At last, she nods. "Alright, then. Here's hoping your new way works and this gets resolved easily. Are you hungry? Bethany made a lot of food, when she heard who exactly Bryce was bringing home."

It doesn't compute for a minute. When she heard Bryce was bringing home a seemingly incompetent witch?

Then it hits me. Oh. When she heard he was bringing home his mate.

Chapter Twenty-Three

Mae

Bryce, it turns out, is a triplet. And second in line for a crown.

I make a mental note not to skip the getting-to-know-you question stage next time, even if the sex is really, really good.

It's very easy to see that they're all siblings. The three men could be the triplets, considering how similar they look, although Celia doesn't look too different from them.

I look at Bryce from the corner of my eye. Even with them looking so similar, I think it's fair to say I got the most attractive one. Something about his eyes, I think.

I learn a little about everyone at the table. Chase is mated to Heath, Bethany to Celia. Callum is still unmated. Each of them works as part of the governing structure of this pack. Bethany is a truly excellent cook, and I wonder if I could convince these people to like me by giving Bethany some enchanted plates that never let food grow cold. That's a spell I know I can do, at least.

"So what took so long?" Heath asks as we all start to slow down on the food. Well, I should say when *they* all start to slow down. They started way before I got here, but take longer to finish. And it's not because they eat slowly, either.

Bethany must have cooked enough to feed an army, and it's barely enough to feed their family.

"Weather delay. Our connecting flight was canceled," Bryce says shortly.

"Shit, and you didn't call me? You know I would have come to get you..." Chase trails off, eyes on me, and I don't know what that's about. "Or, you know. Whatever you worked out instead was fine, probably, I bet." Oh, He knows exactly what we did last night, then.

I refuse to blush. I'm not ashamed of having sex with the hot werewolf who practically threw himself at me. And when they go around introducing people as their mates, I can get a pretty good idea of what they get up to together all on my own.

So I won't be ashamed. Not even when I think, from the knowing looks around the table, that everyone here fully knows I'll fuck him again before I leave.

I look at him out of the corner of my eye, only to find him watching me back, his plate forgotten. The way he's staring at me makes me feel like he's already started to undress me, at least in his mind. Like he's already touching me, slowly, skillfully.

Yeah. Definitely going to fuck him again before I leave. Probably more than once.

I look back down at my plate. The first step is admitting you have a problem, I suppose.

"I don't want to waste any time," I say, interrupting whatever energy is going around this table. I look at Bryce. "Will you show me where the boundary is?"

He nods, and pushes his chair back, then actually holds his hand out to me, like he's going to help me out of my chair.

I raise an eyebrow at him, debate for half a second, but give him my hand. It'd look bad if I didn't, I reason.

Someone—I refuse to look and see who—sniggers as we leave the house.

***

"This is it," Bryce says, gesturing to the wide-open clearing in the middle of the woods.

The woods. Gods, and I thought making a day trip up to Central Park meant a lot of trees.

"This is the spot where a human got through," he says, not noticing my distraction. "It circles the whole village, technically. We can walk the whole thing, but it'll take a while." He makes a gesture, as if indicating the path the border takes, cutting further into the woods.

I force myself to focus. Trees are nice, but they didn't fly me out here to look at trees. They flew me out here to fix my colossal fuck up. "No, this is a good place to start," I say, kneeling down into the dirt, glad I wore pants today. More cover for my knees, and no spontaneous upskirt views for the horny werewolf.

Judging by Bryce's low rumble, the skin-tight pants provide a pretty good view all on their own.

There's an energy here, a sort of mystic buzzing that's not too different to the shop. I let it draw me closer, until I find a rock pressed into the ground. It's not different from any other, gray and lopsided and absolutely average looking, but I can feel Greta's magic in it. Like touching a live wire, the current runs through the rock and gives me a little shock.

"Okay, are there more of these?" I ask, mostly to myself, but Bryce is listening. "Rocks?"

"Magic rocks." I look, standing up so I can walk along the path Bryce indicated earlier. Sure enough, I can follow the current of Greta's magic and find another stone not thirty paces away. "Gods, this must have taken her forever when she first did it," I mutter, hoping I don't have to go through all that. If I'm re-creating this spell from scratch, will I need to lay out every single stone again?

I'll literally never leave this place.

But as I keep walking forward and find another stone, it's immediately apparent that there's still some sort of magical current in these stones. With any luck, they're still usable.

Right. I need to think about this. I don't know exactly how Greta did the spell. Most of the notes in the margins make no sense without knowing the context of the rest of the spell, but the parts I do understand talk about leaving part of yourself in the place and the spell taking a huge amount of energy.

I look around at all the damn rocks Greta must have enchanted and placed, still buzzing with her magic. Yeah. Talk about leaving a part of yourself somewhere.

I turn to Bryce. "Guess what?" I tell him, trying to seem upbeat, like I have this well under control. "Turns out we're taking that walk after all."

CHAPTER TWENTY-FOUR

BRYCE

Those shoes of hers are not meant for walking through the uneven ground of the woods, but she doesn't complain.

Maybe it's the immortal thing—we tend to be hardy, immune to minor aches and pains. Or maybe she's just so used to wearing them, stomping her way around New York.

Whatever it is, they give her just enough height to remind me how truly small she is, create enough noise in the woods to scare off any creatures who weren't already scared by me, and make her ass look fantastic.

Paired with those pants, I can't quite take my eyes off of her. I'm lucky a tree branch doesn't hit me in the face.

"What exactly are you looking for?" I ask as she bends down to investigate what is, by my count, the hundredth rock we've passed.

She looks up at me like she genuinely forgot I was here for a moment, which I would take offense to if I didn't also love the cute furrow in her brow when she's concentrating on the damn rocks. "Have you ever known a witch to talk about their spellwork?" she asks.

"I don't know many witches." True. They don't tend to come out to our village, and while I've of course met some over the years, I've never known them to form any sort of coalition significant enough that we'd need to have diplomatic relations with them. Witches, from what I know, like to be left to their own devices, and we've been happy to let them.

She sighs. "Yeah, not surprised. Look, we are jealous, protective things, alright? The only way you'll get most witches to give you their spells is by pulling their fingernails out with rusty pliers." She stops. "Actually, I definitely know a few witches who would rather take torture than give up their spells."

"Why?" I ask, genuinely interested. Partially—mostly—because I'm desperate to know more about my mate, any information I can get. But also because that is the absolute opposite of pack life, and I can't quite imagine it.

She shrugs. "It's just how we are. I've never known it any other way. If I had to guess? Our spells are our way of life. We don't have claws or supernatural strength. Our spells nourish us and make our lives easier, but they're also our protection and our defense. And if everyone had it, then it wouldn't be great protection anymore." She turns back to the rock. "But that's just a guess. Mostly, I think we're just selfish at this point."

Selfish. "How does that track with you getting that shop? Or leaving it with that demon?"

"Half-demon," she corrects, still looking at the rock. "Violet is half-demon. Half-witch. They probably want to work at that shop a thousand times more than I do."

Right. But if witches are inherently selfish and territorial, then Mae never would have given the shop to them, even temporarily. "And Greta leaving the shop to you?"

She touches the rock, sighs, stands up, and starts walking again, presumably looking for the next one.

"Greta always looked out for me," she says, just as soon as I think she isn't going to explain anymore. "She's my cousin. She, Clay, and I grew up together. Well. Clay's about fifteen years older than me. Greta's like seventy years older than that. But our mothers were sisters. So Greta made sure Clay and I were looked after."

"Looked after?" My protective instincts rise to the front, raring to take action, to do something.

"Not in the literal sense. My mom took care of me. Food on the table, roof over my head. She even sent me to school. And Greta's and Clay's families did the same, as far as I know. But she wasn't going to share her magic. So Greta figured some of it out, and made sure Clay and I figured out the rest." She finally turns to me and shrugs. "I don't know why Greta could share when my own mother couldn't, but she did. And then she opened the shop when I was a kid, and now I'm stuck with it."

"Not Clay?" Why did Greta insist Mae take her shop, if she didn't even want it?

Do I imagine the tension in Mae's spine?

"Greta was getting fifty-fifty odds on her pet projects being successful," is all she says. "So, lucky me. The success story." She huffs. "Some success story."

I do not like that tone. "What do you mean by that?"

She stops at yet another rock. "Greta did some pretty cool magic. Like this—this is really amazing. Wherever she dug this spell up from, it's a powerful piece of magic. Must've taken a lot. And she kept it up for years."

I know, logically, that the border spell is relatively powerful. It's certainly important to our village, especially with the rise of humans snooping around places they have no business being. But the way she talks about it, the sheer awe in her voice, is a level I'll never quite reach.

"I like to do stimulant spells, and enchant my clothes, and figure out little things," she says. "I like my magic for me and my life. Practical stuff. This is all beyond me."

She studies each rock like it'll help her unearth the secrets of life, like it's whispering hidden knowledge to her. Without her sharing, I would never guess that she considers all this beyond her.

"I think the magic you do is pretty impressive," I tell her.

"You're easy to please."

No one in my entire life before her has accused me of that. I shrug. "I still think it's true."

"And I think you're way too easy to talk to," she says, which fills me with an indescribable, giddy warmth. Giddy. Me.

My mate thinks I'm easy to talk to. My mate wants to talk to me about the things that are on her mind.

"How far around are we?" she asks, looking at yet another rock.

"A little less than halfway." I look at the sky. "Sunset is in an hour. Want to start fresh in the morning?"

Her whole body seems to deflate. "I guess so. Sorry I don't have an answer for you yet."

Like I could ever be sorry my mate has reason to stick around a little longer. It's just more time to woo her with.

Gods, if Celia could hear inside my brain, she'd beat me over the head. And I'd deserve it. I know the border spell is important, and that we need it working again as quickly as possible. And that hoping it'll take longer so I have more time to convince Mae to give us a chance is just me failing the pack.

The spell will get done. I fully believe it, fully trust Mae's ability to do it.

But in the meantime, I'm going to take advantage of every single second I get with her.

CHAPTER TWENTY-FIVE

MAE

He takes me to his house.

I probably should have thought about that sooner. That every time the big werewolf talked about taking me home, he meant it literally. Not just his town, no. His house.

Oh gods, it's his town too, isn't it? Not in the same way New York is my city. It's his town because he is second in line for a godsdamn crown. He owns this town, basically.

And he owns this house. This house that is way too fucking big for one person. This house with a kitchen the size of my apartment, where Bryce is currently puttering around, putting the final touches on dinner.

A dinner he wouldn't let me help prepare, I might add, even though I caved and admitted to him I'd been a line cook for five years once. And after admitting to the thousand-year-old werewolf prince, who is apparently a diplomat for his entire species, that I've had something as plebeian as a regular job, he just told me I was his guest.

So now I'm sipping wine—that he definitely did not pick up at a grocery store—out of a big glass, sitting at his counter, and watching him cook.

A part of me wonders if this is his attempt to prove something to me. That he's good for more than just fingering me in public restrooms. That he's the type of guy someone could build a life with.

But then I don't let myself wonder about it, because if I do, then I'll get stuck on it. He's not wrong, is the thing. This is definitely the kind of guy who you build a life with, with a nice home and fancy wine and comfortable dinners.

And probably toe-curling sex after.

And he's also a prince of werewolves with some sort of destined job, and I'm me. The witch who works as a line cook and a tailor and a secretary and a million other odds-and-ends jobs over the years, who can't keep her shop open and still dreams of the pages of atlases.

Yeah, right. He's the type of guy I could build a life with in my dreams, and I need to remember that. Dreams stay in the night, and that's all.

He places a heaping plate of pasta in front of me, grates cheese freshly over the top, and pours me more wine before I know what's going on. "You cook a lot?" I ask.

He shrugs. "Not recently. I've been traveling a lot. So I've been eating in restaurants, or room service, that type of thing."

Right. Because he travels to represent his pack. I'm glad for the continued reality check.

"You? I know you said you cooked professionally, but do you like it?"

I think of the amount of nights I've eaten instant noodles lately. "When I have time." That's a pleasant way to put it.

I take a bite. Damn, he can really cook.

When reminding myself why this seduction tactic cannot work is clearly becoming entirely ineffective, I turn to safer ground, and bring attention back to the whole reason I'm here in the first place. "So, we pick up the same place we left off tomorrow?"

He shrugs. "I'm following your lead."

That sounds almost like a dismissal. I bite my lip. "You don't have to, you know, follow me around again. I'm sure I can figure it out."

He gapes at me for a moment. It's honestly a charming look on him, to see him a little out of his element, a little thrown. But he recovers quickly. "First off, if today was the first time you've wandered through an actual forest, I'm not letting you just figure it out tomorrow." Okay, not an unfair point. "And second, I don't have to do anything, but I promise you, I really want to be following you around. Everywhere."

I try to get a look into his eyes, expecting to see a leer there, the way he looks at my body to let me know he's interested. I expect a double entendre about my ass, which he seems to like. But it's not there.

All that's there is raw sincerity. He likes spending time with me. It makes something warm bloom within me.

I nod and need a swallow of wine to be able to speak again. "Alright. Uh, start at the same place, then." And I have no idea what I'll find there. But I'll just have to figure it out.

"Good," he murmurs. "First thing after breakfast, then." He smiles a bit and uses his chin to point into the kitchen. "Coffee machine is right there."

He remembered. "Thank you."

"You done with that?" he asks, gesturing to my plate.

I look down, and it's indeed empty. "Yeah. You cooked, so I'll wash."

"No."

I cock my head. "No?"

"I cooked dinner. You take care of dessert."

I reach for my wine again, having a feeling about where this is going, and it's making something inside me flutter. "What do you want for dessert?"

"I think you know," he says, voice getting lower and lower with each word.

Then, like a flash, he's out of his chair and in front of mine, pulling me until I'm standing, then continuing to pull until I wrap my legs around his waist, my arms around his neck, and kiss him hard.

"You taste good." His voice is a rumble against my mouth, making me shiver, making me want more. "Can I have you for dessert, pretty little witch?"

I don't hesitate. I should, I shouldn't let us get any deeper, and—

"Yes," I say, kissing him again, not letting myself think about it any further.

He growls and I swallow the sound. Then, all too soon, he's breaking the kiss, and I can't bite back the whine fast enough to stop it. But all he does is smile and kiss my throat before laying me onto the kitchen table, tugging a chair up between my thighs. Without waiting for him, I scramble at my shirt, then the bra underneath it, wanting them gone, wanting to feel that little electric pulse across my skin when he stares at me with those hungry eyes.

He doesn't disappoint, smiling disbelievingly as he carefully works my pants down my hips. I wiggle to try to help him, probably just making it worse, but eventually I'm completely naked, completely exposed for his eyes.

"Godsdamn gorgeous," he rasps, his hands making slow paths up and down my inner thighs. He nudges them a little further apart each time, just slightly, as if he has all the time in the world. As if these little touches and looks are enough for right now.

His hands drift higher and higher up my thighs, a tease, and I cave first, unable to suppress a whine. "C'mon, don't you want dessert?" I taunt, trying to draw him into doing something.

He growls and leans down towards my already-wet cunt, not wasting a second longer.

His lips latch around my clit, sucking and teasing while I throw my head back and rock against his face, already desperate for more.

I've had more sex in the last two days than I've had in the last year, and I'm already humping his face like I'm desperate and have never had an orgasm before. What is with this guy?

A thousand years' worth of practice, I remind myself hazily as I continue to rock, my fingers finding purchase in his hair. That has to count for something.

"You taste so damn sweet," he rumbles against the soft skin of my inner thigh, sending shivers crashing through me, making me bite my lip so I don't moan too loud.

Then I remember that, for the first time in my life, there are no neighbors right through the wall. The closest neighbor is a hundred yards or more away, and Bryce is making me want to moan.

I let go.

"That's it." His voice is practically just a hum of approval, vibrating against my folds, making me gasp. "That's it, little witch, Mae, let go and enjoy it—"

How could I ever do anything but enjoy this? He bites lightly at my clit as a reward when I moan, then licks through my folds, like I'm a delicacy he wants to taste.

"Bryce—"

The rumble against my skin is enough to tell me how he feels about me saying his name, and I can't help it, saying it again, high and choked.

He grabs my hips with both hands, angling me so I'm supporting my weight on my upper back and he has a better, deeper angle, driving his tongue into me, holding me to his face like he's afraid he'll lose me otherwise. I gasp at the new angle, the new access it offers him, and hold his hair tighter.

The two of us, holding each other in place, like either of us are going to leave this position right now.

I feel it building, rocking my hips against his face to chase the feeling. "Bryce, Bryce I—"

He rumbles against me, returns his focus entirely to my clit, and grips my hips so tight I wouldn't be shocked to find bruises.

And under his attention, I come. I writhe against his face, shaking, completely out of control, trusting him to hold me as I chase the orgasm and moan. He keeps sucking through it, as if daring me to go over again, pushing for more.

When I can think clearly—in the loosest sense of the term—I push his head back, gently. He growls, but lets me go.

I'm going to come again tonight, but it won't be on his tongue.

I'd tell him that. I'd take action, get him as naked as me or relocate to his lap, but I can't stop my shaking.

Then I watch Bryce pull back enough to lick the wetness from his face, an obscene, obvious show just for me. "I'd like to end every meal this way." His voice is little more than a rasp, and it makes me shiver all over again.

I ignore the every meal comment, ignore how few meals we likely have left together. I can't focus on it, anyway. All I can think about is getting him out of his clothes, getting him inside me. Making him come.

"Show me your bed," I command, and he's on his feet, lifting me up into his arms before I can blink.

Chapter Twenty-Six

Bryce

She feels so good in my arms, all soft curves and warmth, every inch of her skin inviting my touch. Someday soon, I'm going to take my time, touch every single inch of her, find every spot on her body that makes her moan.

It's not easy to walk up the stairs, as hard as I am, but thinking about getting her into bed, thinking about sinking into her tight, warm cunt, is motivation enough to try.

I bring her to the bed and lay her down, taking a moment to step back and look, really look, taking it all in.

Her. Here. In my bed.

Our bed? The thought feels so right, so necessary, that I immediately accept it. Our bed.

As if my staring encourages her, she spreads her thighs, showing me her damp curls. She gives me a wicked smile, and I can't help myself anymore.

"Tell me what you want tonight." I'll give her anything she asks for.

"Take your clothes off." With pleasure. A button rips off my shirt as I yank it over my head, not giving a flying fuck where it lands or even if the shirt survives.

Because when I shove my pants down, and when she stares at my cock, hard just for her, desperate and waiting for her, I know that her eyes on me are the only thing in the entire universe that matters.

She stares at me like she's hungry for me, like she wants to pounce on me, and I wait, muscles coiled and ready to move, ready to go wherever she leads.

"Come here, lie down," she offers, sitting up and petting the bed next to her.

I scramble to do what she says, practically falling onto the bed next to her. "What do you have in mind?" I ask, propping myself on an elbow to watch her.

And gods, what a sight she is.

She puts her hand on the center of my chest to push me back. I let her, because I want to be wherever she wants me to be, and the look of concentration on her face is stunning, but the reality is someone with her strength couldn't really hope to push a werewolf around.

Then again, here she is, exactly as strong as she is, and easily pushing me around, anyway. My little witch, damn powerful and strong.

When I'm on my back, she clambers on top of me, swinging her legs over my hips, resting her hot core dangerously close to my cock.

Fuck. I need Mae to have mercy on me. She's come once tonight already, and once this morning, but I've been aching for her all day.

Her smile is dangerous, and if it weren't for the hand still on my chest, I'd sit up to kiss it from her mouth. My hands automatically move to her hips. "What's your plan, wicked witch?" I ask, stroking my thumbs along the soft skin there.

"I'm going to make you come," she promises me.

I can't help but laugh. "Mae, you could make me come by breathing on me right now. I'm looking for something more specific than that."

Her nails dig into my chest lightly, and I arch up into the touch. "I'm going to ride your cock until you come, specific enough?"

Deliciously so. Agonizingly, deliciously so. I stroke her hip bones again. "Need any help?"

She raises an eyebrow. "I think I can find your cock without help. It's fucking big enough." And, without giving me time to respond, she raises herself over me, grabs my cock, and guides it into her welcoming, hot cunt.

She throws her head back as she slides down me, and I'm torn between watching the long, beautiful line of her neck or watching where I disappear inside her.

I'm so deep in her, and her cunt clenches around me, warm and dripping. It takes everything in me to lie still, to let her set the pace like she so clearly wants.

She takes a long moment, getting used to the stretch, then rolls her hips in tiny little circles, teasing both of us. She bites her lip. "Don't hold back now," I admonish her, because she sounded so fucking beautiful earlier, moaning with my head between her thighs. Because I made her feel good, and she was so damn beautiful and let me hear how good it was for her. "Let me hear you."

She looks down at me now and seems to stare into my soul for a long moment before she nods. Almost as soon as she does, she rocks her hips again, that teasing, maddening little swirl, just enough to make me nearly frenzied for her.

I want to hear her moan. I want to drive her wild; I want to make her come. I grip her hips tighter, with half a mind to move her myself, but she takes it out of my hands and raises until I'm barely inside of her before sliding down me once more, punching a moan out of both of us.

Gods above, she feels so damn good. I gasp out her name as she does it again, and again, until the room is filled with a litany of her breathy little moans, and our hips slapping together, and me moaning her name.

I can feel my orgasm building, my balls tightening, the wolf inside me roaring to change positions and claim our witch.

"Mae, I—"

"Bryce, I'm so damn close," she gasps. "I—I need—"

I take one hand off her hip and find her clit, applying just a little pressure, but she moans louder than I've heard her yet. Her rhythm falters, but just for a second, and she valiantly picks it back up as I rub in slow, steady circles.

My own hips are moving now. I can't stop them, can't lie still when my own orgasm is so damn close, when I can feel it, when her cunt is squeezing me and I just need—

"Oh—oh gods, Bryce, I—"

Her hips stutter, then stop, her words getting cut off into a breathy moan as she comes.

That's all it takes. Her cunt squeezes me and I lose control entirely, fucking my hips upward erratically as I come inside her. My vision goes fuzzy around the edges, but I never lose sight of her, glorious and everything I've ever hoped for.

"Gods, you're good at that," I tell her when I feel like I can breathe again. I don't sound like myself, not really. Maybe this is the version of me that exists in a world where I get fucked stupid by my mate.

By my mate. My beautiful, fucking perfect mate who just rode me to what has to inarguably be the best orgasm of my life. So far, anyway, because if I have anything to say about it, there will be many, many more to come.

She doesn't respond, just grins and then leans down to kiss me. I push myself onto my elbows, wanting to be closer, meeting her halfway. She moans against my mouth, biting my bottom lip as she kisses me.

This isn't a soft kiss, not some post-orgasm kiss to tell me she enjoyed herself. No, this is still hungry and hot, and I find myself wanting to respond, even when I know that's out of the question right now.

"Aren't you tired?" I ask her, sitting up and adjusting her so she's sitting on my lap, smiling as she wiggles in my lap, very clearly not tired. "You'd think I didn't make you come twice tonight."

"No," she says. "I feel great. Super energized..." She trails off.

"What is it?"

"How soon do you think you can go again?" she asks me.

I try to give her a look. A look that says, *are you kidding me?* A look that says, *you know full well that's not happening yet.*

Somehow, though, what comes out of my mouth is, "Where do you want me?"

Chapter Twenty-Seven

Mae

Greta said the spell takes energy and a piece of yourself. I don't know if this is how she intended the comment, but if I was energy right now, I'd be a damn nuclear reactor.

My veins are full of fire, and I feel more alive than I have in a long, long time. I have to know.

Bryce isn't as enthusiastic when I drag him out of bed and demand he take me back to the middle of the woods. I don't know if it's the fact that I promised him sex and now look like I want to go hiking, or if it's demanding we put on clothes, or if it's the fact that it's now comfortably well after dark. But he's a good sport about it.

If it's the mate thing, it's working in my favor and I try not to think about it.

The trees around us make spooky sounds this late at night, and my night vision isn't much better than the average human's. Every sound makes me jump.

Bryce puts his hand on the small of my back, warm and big and oddly comforting. "I'm the scariest thing out here," he reminds me, voice a reassuring rumble. "And that's an owl. It won't hurt you."

Right. I try to take comfort in that, that I have a big bad werewolf trailing after me, ready to defend me. And I get myself calm, until he nudges me with his hip. "Besides, don't witches like owls, anyways?"

"That is a stereotype." I manage to sound indignant as I say it, but the truth is, most witches I know do tend to like the stereotypical witchy pets. Maybe because they're all solitary creatures, like us.

I wouldn't mind a cat, but I've never seen an owl in my life.

"My mistake," he says grandly, then takes the opportunity to lean over and place a kiss on the top of my head.

We return to one of Greta's many stones. It's not the one we left off on earlier, but it really doesn't matter. The stones are a circle with no beginning and no end, and every one of them hums with Greta's spell.

And soon, they'll hum with mine.

"What exactly do you want out here?" he asks me.

"I want you to fuck me, and fuck me hard," I tell him. I suppose there's nothing that says it has to be hard. Hell, there's nothing that specifically says Greta meant fucking, and I hope she initially didn't, because I don't want to think about her out in these woods with someone. But I know how alive I'll feel if he fucks me hard. How energetic. How powerful.

He raises an eyebrow. "And it had to be out here?"

"I thought wolves like fucking in the woods?" I tease.

He grumbles, "That's a stereotype," but before I can say anything about that, he's already grabbed my head to kiss me fiercely, moving us until my back is against a tree.

One of his hands migrates from my hair to the hem of my shirt, working his way under it and finding my chest. He groans, squeezing my tit as he rocks against me.

I can feel him getting hard against me, already ready to go again. I groan, trailing one hand down his chest and finding his cock through his pants, giving it a squeeze.

He breaks the kiss to stop me. "Don't do that," he warns, voice barely more than a rasp. "Not if you want me to get to the fucking you hard stage."

I let go of his cock and instead grab for the button on his pants. "Then let's move along."

"Impatient witch."

"Are you complaining?" I get his pants open, shoving my hand inside. No underwear. Excellent.

"Never." His hands move back to my shirt, this time pulling at the hem and taking it back off me. I push at his pants, trying to get them down his hips, and after a moment, manage to succeed.

He rips his own shirt off over his head while I take care of my pants, cursing myself for dragging them back on. Yes, they look fantastic, and yes, I picked them for a reason this morning. But they seem immensely impractical for getting fucked in the woods tonight.

Eventually though, we're both naked, out here under the trees and the stars above. I shiver, but not from the cold. I've never been so exposed before.

But Bryce's eyes are alight with something deep and primal, and he's back in my space, hauling me close so there's not an inch between us before I can speak. "You're the most beautiful thing I've ever seen, Mae."

I don't know what to say to that. Don't know how to respond. Who says that to someone? He's a thousand years old; how can he mean that?

He's the most beautiful thing I've seen too, I think, and I have to fight myself not to say it.

Luckily, I don't need to think of a response, because Bryce picks me up by the hips, dragging me up his body, so I wrap my legs around his hips for support.

"Fuck you hard, you said?" he asks, face buried in my neck, the vibrations making me shiver.

I manage a nod, hands going around his shoulders to clasp at his back, dragging him to me like I'm afraid he'll leave. "Hard as you can manage."

All of a sudden I find myself against a tree, being lifted just enough for him to line his cock up with my entrance.

I throw my head back against the tree and let out a long moan as he slides into me. It shouldn't feel this good, shouldn't feel like my cunt is some sort of lightning rod. But I feel every thrust like electricity through me.

I moan loud enough that I probably scare away everything that might still be in the woods, and I drag my fingernails across his shoulders, which just seems to push him harder into me.

"Fucking beautiful witch. Am I giving you what you want, Mae?"

"Y—oh, gods, yes," I manage, wrapping my legs impossibly tighter around him, trying to pull him deeper.

"Are you going to come for me?" he demands.

I could, in a heartbeat. I just need—

He moves one hand from my hip to my clit, and all it takes is two strokes to drive me right over the edge.

He follows me, making a noise loud enough to deafen the rest of the forest, and I worry for half a second we'll fall. He doesn't let me go, though, holding us upright even as he shakes from the force of it.

And then he kisses my neck, soft and gentle, the complete opposite of what we just did. "Was that what you wanted, Mae?"

I'm wrapped in a layer of bliss, high on my orgasm, and it takes me an embarrassingly long moment to remember that there was a reason I made him fuck me in the woods in the middle of the night.

But I feel alive, I think. More full of energy than I can ever remember being, like it might somehow explode out of me.

Like I need to find somewhere to put it.

I wiggle until he puts me down. "Let's find out," I say, walking on unsteady legs over to the stone, feeling his come drip down my thigh, a gross, delicious reminder of why exactly I feel like I can take on the world right now.

I feel him coming up behind me, but I'm entirely focused on the spell, on the hunk of stone in the ground I'm hoping I can pour a whole lot of magic into.

I crouch down next to the rock and place both hands on top of it, feeling Greta's spell and trying to interweave my own magic, my own intentions, into it.

And then I begin to sing.

Just softly, more humming than singing most of the time, although the occasional word does slip in. I don't know the song, never have, but it always comes back to me when I'm trying to cast my spells.

It's like the words for the spell are buried somewhere in that song, like I somehow know them deep in my bones. And this time is no different from any other. The stone under my hands begins to glow, and a quick glance confirms the two nearest me in either direction are also glowing.

126

"Gods, you're doing it," Bryce whispers, and I ignore him entirely, continuing to hum.

And I keep going until it feels like the words run out, and the energy fades from my body. I hum one final bar, mostly nonsense now, and almost collapse like my strings have been cut.

Bryce catches me, and I realize uncomfortably that I expected him to. That, after two days, I somehow expected him to be there for me, ready, anticipating my needs.

And now I realize that I better train myself out of that habit quickly, because I've done it. I've done the spell. I've done what I was brought here to do, and the only thing left to do is go home.

Bryce doesn't seem to be thinking that far ahead, though, because he's stroking his hands up and down my arms, letting me rest against his chest. "You're okay," he murmurs. "You're okay."

I am so much better than okay. The magic I just did was powerful, and raw, and honestly so much more than I ever thought I could do.

"I did it," I mumble to him, turning my face to look at him.

He kisses the top of my head. "You're damn right you did. I knew you would."

I want to tell him he has too much confidence in me, that this mate thing really fucked with his head. But then again, aren't we here because of his confidence in me?

Well. That and how good we are at fucking, I guess.

My whole body feels tired and sore now, but nothing more so than my cunt, still dripping with his come and swollen from two rough poundings in one night. It's slightly painful but also ridiculously perfect.

It's a feeling I very firmly tell myself not to get used to.

Chapter Twenty-Eight

Bryce

There's a moment both Celia and Heath have described to me, where you go from loving your mate because they're your mate, to loving them entirely because they're them. And I think I just crossed that moment.

I don't think I ever saw anything more attractive than her crouching in the woods, generating power for a spell from fucking me. Even the somewhat creepy humming was spellbinding.

I want this witch forever. I want Mae for every moment for the rest of our long lives.

For now, I settle for holding her while her body shivers. When she seems to settle a little more solidly into her skin, I kiss her ear and say, "Want to go back?"

The rocks aren't glowing anymore, so there's nothing left to watch. There's not even any wildlife left around to listen to; we clearly scared them all away.

She nods, so I help her to her feet and move to find our clothes. But she snatches my shirt from me and puts it on her, clearly in no hurry to put on any of her own clothes, holding them in a bundle at her side.

She gives me a look that challenges me to argue, which is the absolute last thing on my mind. Mostly, I'm just thinking about how adorable she is. How that shirt somehow makes me want to fuck her again, even if there's no way I'm managing three times in one night.

I tug on my pants and hold out my arm to her. "Hold onto me," I tell her. "It's dark and I see better than you out here. Unless you want me to carry you?"

She takes my arm and I try not to be disappointed that she won't let me carry her.

***

When we emerge from the forest, Chase, Heath, and Callum are all waiting for us, arms crossed. Callum has a sword at his side.

"What?" I snap, in absolutely no mood to talk to them when I just want to get Mae back to our house and back to bed.

Chase grins. "Full moon come early?"

I snarl, but it's not like it's exactly hard to tell what we got up to in the forest. Mae's wearing my shirt. *My* ripped shirt. And she has a leaf in her hair.

"What are you doing here?"

"You kidding? That light show woke all of us up," Callum says. "We said we'd check it out."

"How brave, waiting for us to come to you," Mae says dryly.

Heath raises an eyebrow. "Well, we did go out to you, but then we started hearing things... not to mention the scent."

I furiously think over our encounter in this new light. Surely I would have heard...

No. Not when the only sound I wanted to listen to was Mae's sweet moans.

"That a normal witch thing?" Chase has the gall to ask. "I know demons don't... you know... glow like that, but maybe witches do. I don't know what other casters do."

"Shut up," I growl at him, because I know Mae gets embarrassed, that she worries people are judging her. And Chase means it as a joke, but Mae should never feel like she'll be judged here. "It was the spell," I tell him, trying to end the conversation.

"Oh, so the sex was celebratory, then?"

Apparently, he's not going to drop it, and I'm not about to explain what happened out there to them, so I just scoop Mae up into my arms and start making my way back to my house. She doesn't protest when I do it, either. She turns her face into my chest, letting me carry her away from my family. "Spread the word that everything's fine, and the spell is done," I tell them, then turn away from them and put them completely out of my mind, focusing only on Mae.

***

She lets me hold her when we sleep. In fact, I might say she initiates it, practically cleaving to me from the moment we get into bed. I welcome every touch, every press of her skin against mine, and sleep better than I have in weeks.

Only to be rudely awakened by a pounding at my front door.

Mae stirs and looks at me blearily. I have to fight the urge to tell her how adorable I'm finding her anti-morning, pre-coffee feelings. Mostly, because I don't think she'll react well to hearing it pre-coffee.

"I'll turn the coffee maker on," I grunt, getting out of bed to pull my pants on. At least this way I can kill two birds with one stone.

And whoever is knocking on my door better have a damn good reason.

I leave them to continue pounding on the door until the coffee is started. Let them suffer; my mate and her coffee addiction come first.

"What do you want?" I'm already halfway through snarling before I even fully open the door, only to find Heath there, looking more than a little exasperated.

"I swear I'll kick your ass from here to next year."

"You can try," he says, annoyingly unruffled by the threat.

"What do you want?"

"Celia says we're having breakfast this morning. All of us."

"Busy."

"I don't think it's optional. We told her about the spell."

I swallow. Right. She's going to want the full report of that.

"I have a phone for a damn reason, you know. You don't need to pound on my door."

"Yeah, see. Phones can be ignored. This way, I know you'll be there."

I run a hand over my face. This is not what I wanted. I wanted to sleep holding Mae as long as possible, and see if she likes the idea of morning sex, and spend the day getting to know her better. Not this.

But an order is an order, and I remind myself that I can't blame Celia for wanting an update on the job we technically hired Mae to do. "Fine."

"Great. I'll wait. We should go over now."

I raise an eyebrow. "If you don't want Mae to turn you into a toad, you'll let her get dressed and have her coffee before you expect us anywhere."

"Can she really do that?"

How the fuck should I know? But it sounds good. "You prepared to find out?"

***

He leaves, thankfully. Which means I can bring the biggest mug I have to Mae, and wake her up slightly more gently than my brother pounding down our door.

She drinks the coffee greedily and all I can do is watch, attention rapt as her throat moves and her eyes slip closed.

"Celia wants everyone at her house for breakfast," I say when I think she's had enough of the coffee to process it.

"Is Bethany cooking again?"

"Most likely." Almost guaranteed. Bethany always cooks.

She looks down at herself, completely naked, my shirt long gone. "I need time to get ready."

"Take all the time you need." I'm not exactly ready for company either, although I think I could be ready to go in five minutes. But I doubt Mae will be that quick.

So she gets out of bed, grabs her bag, and goes to the bathroom.

The water in the shower starts. I frown, thinking of her naked and wet, but I wasn't invited, so I content myself with finding my own clean clothes and thinking of whatever scandalously wonderful outfit Mae will put on today.

***

Her clothes absolutely destroy anything I could have imagined and stop me dead in my tracks. She's wearing a dress, only the skirt is basically two panels held together with crisscrossing straps well up to her waistline, revealing all of her beautiful legs and hips. I want to bite between those straps, lick and kiss there until she's squirming and begging me to stick my head under that skirt—

"Ready for breakfast?" she asks, sliding her big boots on.

How the hell I'm supposed to be ready for breakfast with my family when I'm thinking of what would happen if that skirt moved just a few inches in either direction—surely she can't be wearing panties, not with her hips completely visible—I don't know. But I nod, and tell myself to get it together.

Chapter Twenty-Nine

Mae

His eyes light up when he sees the dress. I don't know why I wore it. I have more conservative things in this bag.

Maybe I just wanted to feel his eyes on me like that one more time. Maybe it's a parting gift for him.

Because the job is over, and that means my reason for being here is over, and everyone at this breakfast but Bryce seems to know it.

I keep a remarkably straight face while giving the bare bones of the spell details to Celia, but of course Chase has to ruin it.

"So like, you're telling me the border spell is secretly some form of sex magic?" he asks. "What, did your cousin just come out here and pick a werewolf to fuck?"

There are a few sputters around the table at that. Quietly, entirely to myself, I concede that could have been completely possible. Werewolves tend to be attractive, from everything I've seen, although I definitely got the best possible option when picking a werewolf sex partner to fuel a spell with.

"I didn't use Greta's spell, just some of her notes. So I have no idea how she powered it."

"So what you're saying is, strong maybe?"

I am absolutely saying that, and I am absolutely not going to say that out loud.

Thankfully, Celia, who seems to have no time for anyone's nonsense, even at the breakfast table, interrupts him. "So it's done now?"

"Yeah, it's done." I suppose technically I can't confirm that for sure, but half the village can apparently confirm the light show, and what else could that mean?

She nods. "Good. I'm glad." I don't miss the unspoken message. She's glad I just fucked up and didn't fuck them over. She's glad I didn't hurt Bryce. She's glad she doesn't have to hurt me. "What's next for you?" she asks.

There it is. I should've known Celia would be the one to get to the point. I take a deep breath. "I guess I go home," I say, bracing myself.

Bryce's fork clatters to his plate. "You don't have to go anywhere."

"I have a business to run." Sort of. A business that barely stays afloat. A business I don't want anything to do with.

But it's my problem, and at least I know the money in the business account is free and clear, so I can start making some business decisions.

And hey, if I can do this kind of spell, maybe I can find some other big-ticket clients. That'll help out.

Bryce's mouth tightens, but he doesn't argue. I guess I appreciate that, because I probably would have cast some sort of awful hex if he implied being his mate meant that my store and my promise to Greta weren't important anymore. That he owned me and my time now that we've had sex.

Was the sex good? The best I've ever had, probably. Absolutely mind-blowing. And still not something I'm giving up everything for.

"Can I fly you home then?" he asks, voice subdued.

"I don't think that's a good idea." Mostly, because if I get him back to New York, I can imagine myself failing to let him go. Best make a clean break of it.

He nods, still not arguing with me. "Can I call you?"

I should tell him no. Should cut this off now, stop whatever we've started here. Where can it go?

But I can't do that. I think about how the thousand year old werewolf looks at me when I wear something that humans my age condemn me for. I think about him bringing me coffee in bed. I think about the intensity in his eyes and the press of his hand on my back.

I try not to, but I think about him fucking me against that tree.

"Yeah," I say. "Of course. Please." I can't keep eye contact, looking down at my plate. "I should probably book a plane ticket."

Chase huffs. "You two really are pathetic. I'll take her."

I bristle at being called pathetic, but can't really argue with it. "I don't need an escort."

"Listen, you have your magic, I have mine. And if you're willing to be a teensy-tiny bit tired later, I can get you there. No plane required."

That sounds like a good deal. "Alright then."

"Great. Get your stuff. I would rather not bop all over the world playing delivery driver today."

"What, now?" Bryce demands gruffly.

Yes, now, I realize. Like ripping a band aid off.

So I nod, and thank Bethany quietly for the food, and move to go get my bag.

Bryce moves so fast to follow me that his chair makes a screeching noise on the floor when he pushes it back.

"I get why you have to go," he says as we leave Celia and Bethany's house. "I do. But I'll... please. Don't shut me out."

"Call me," I tell him. It won't be more than that. I can't do more than that.

"I will."

He follows me up to the bedroom to grab my bag, but immediately distracts me by pinning me to the wall to kiss me senseless.

We return to Chase and the others with my bag and my hair significantly messier than when we started. I ignore their looks. I ignore Bryce too, because I can't say goodbye again, and reach out for Chase. "Let's go."

He grabs my arm and then we're gone, appearing in my shop before I even know what's happening.

Violet looks up at us with wide eyes. Chase gives me a mocking bow. "Take care of yourself," he says, and then he's gone.

Leaving me all alone, back in my shop in New York. Exactly where I wanted to be.

CHAPTER THIRTY

MAE

Violet gives me an unimpressed look as soon as he's gone. "It go well?" They ask.

I bite my lip. "It went... yeah. Fine. Did the spell. Money's all set." I look sidelong at them. "It's enough for you to keep the job part-time. For now. I can't promise I'll be able to forever." I run a hand through my still-mussed hair. "Maybe if I can get more big jobs..."

"I can help you find those," Violet says.

"What?"

They shrug. "I hear things."

I want to ask if they mean that in a gossipy way, or in a voices in their head way. Maybe they're actually a seer.

I've never met a half witch, half demon before Violet. The magic is bound to interact in interesting ways.

"That would be great," I manage, and don't let myself think about those big jobs. What if they're just more spells that I don't know how to do?

I shake myself. I'll figure it out. I did it before, and I can do it again.

"I re-organized the displays," Violet says, and a quick look around tells me it's true. They don't sound apologetic about it in the slightest, either. "It should be more visually appealing to customers now."

I don't know how true that is, but I'm not going to complain. "Alright. Alright, good. Let me put my bag upstairs. Then I'll be down to help out."

***

"Clay's come by every day you've been gone," Violet tells me as soon as I come back downstairs.

I freeze. "And you're waiting until now to tell me?"

They shrug. "You looked like you had a lot on your mind. And he hasn't done anything. He mostly stands at the door and tells me to invite him in. Which I don't do, obviously. And then he tries some spell—haven't figured out what yet—but it never seems to work, so he just leaves."

I hate every piece of that information. "Good thing I'm back," I murmur. "He been by today yet?"

"Still early," Violet says, shrugging, then leaves the register to once again go mess around with the crystal display.

***

Clay's continued obnoxious pursuit is a thorn in my side, but he really doesn't have anything over me. I offered him the spell books for a translation he didn't even do correctly. I did the spell completely on my own, so I am one hundred percent free and clear from owing him anything.

Which is great. I'm getting a feeling Clay is a bad witch to owe something to.

I don't know what he's gotten himself involved in, or why he's so insistent on getting Greta's shop. But Violet wasn't exaggerating when they said he comes by every day. About two hours after I arrive home, he's knocking on our door.

I don't open it. It's unlocked, considering it's the middle of business hours, and if he really wanted to, he could walk right in. "Get lost!" I shout through the glass.

"Cousin, lovely to see you back. Let's catch up."

"Let's not. Fuck off."

And then, bizarrely, he seems to mutter a spell, and, when nothing happens, he turns around and leaves.

I blink at the spot on the sidewalk where he just stood. "What the fuck?"

Violet looks up. "Yeah, I told you. Weird, right?"

It's bizarre, and I have absolutely no idea what to do about it, about him.

***

I don't miss Bryce until I go upstairs to go to bed.

I slept so well last night once we got back from our impromptu late night fuck in the woods. And I slept well in the hotel the night before that too. He's warm, and big, and cuddling him feels like being completely surrounded, like absolutely nothing can touch me while I sleep.

Compared to that, my bed feels cold and empty. It feels too vulnerable, honestly. Which is rich, because before now I always considered sleeping with someone else to be the vulnerable option. But no. Bryce is safe in a way I never expected to want or need, and now, without him, I feel the distinct lack of it.

I grit my teeth and turn over. It was only two nights. I'll get used to sleeping without him. I have to.

CHAPTER THIRTY-ONE

BRYCE

I make it three days before I call her. And I only make it that long because the entire family keeps me busy, inventing tasks for me to keep my mind off Mae.

They fail utterly, of course, but I appreciate the effort.

But at the end of the third day, I can't wait any longer. I need to hear her voice.

She picks up on the second ring. "Hello?"

My throat goes dry and everything I ever wanted to say to her fades. Did I once consider myself good at this? At talking to people, and at talking to people I wanted to seduce in particular?

"Hey, it's me. Bryce."

There's a shuffling sound, like moving papers. "Hey, Bryce. How are you?"

"Did I call at a bad time?"

"What I'm learning is there are no good times when you're trying to keep a business afloat. This time is as good as any."

"The business still isn't doing well?" I ask, which is absolutely not the question I wanted to ask, and not the tone I wanted to take. The last thing I want is her to think I'm accusing her of something.

She sighs. "Rent is astronomical and products like we have aren't cheap and it turns out Greta had been buying a lot of it on credit for a while. So, I'm digging out of that hole. Plus I want to keep Violet as an employee. And right now I have them part-time, but they should really have full-time work and I'm not sure how I'm going to swing a full-time salary. And they don't really need health insurance, so I dodged a bullet there, but—" She cuts herself off. "You don't care about this."

"I do," I tell her immediately. "Keep talking."

"Why on earth would you care about this?"

Because it's on her mind. Because she cares about it. That's all I've ever needed to care about what she says.

"So what's the plan?" I ask her instead of answering.

"Honestly? Violet and I are planning to look to see if there are any more big spell jobs."

"Well, you'll be the first person we hire forevermore," I promise her.

She actually laughs at that, and it makes the wolf inside me curl up, delighted and content to hear it. "That sounds like a conflict of interest."

"Why? Because you're my mate? You should know for wolves, that's not a conflict of interest, it's just common sense to trust a wolf's mate above anyone else. Besides, they all saw the light show from your spell. They were impressed. We know you're the best."

She's quiet for a long second. "I'm really not. I appreciate the vote of confidence and everything, but I'm not the best. I'm very, *very* average."

"Agree to disagree." What are other witches doing if she's just average?

"No, like, it's an indisputable fact—forget it. You wouldn't understand."

"Nope. I don't understand how you're not the most impressive witch I've ever seen," I tell her.

"You're a flirt," she accuses, but I think she's smiling on the other end of the call. "Why'd you call?"

"I wanted to hear your voice," I tell her, but the truth is so much more than that. I feel like I can't sleep without her, like I'm missing a limb. Like the world is a little duller. Like whatever cheer I managed to scrape together with her around is gone now.

My family has kept me busy, but their little tasks and distractions can't go on forever. And Celia will have actual work for me soon, but I worry I won't be at my best for that either.

I called her because I need her. Maybe selfishly, I called to see if she missed me at all.

But I don't ask that. That would be selfish, and as much as I want to be, I can't be selfish with her.

She's silent for a long moment, but then she says it, what I wanted to hear and didn't dare hope for. "I've missed you."

My breath catches and it feels like it takes a long moment to get my lungs working correctly again. "Yeah?"

"Yeah. How often do you come out to New York for pack business?"

Almost never. But I'll find something. Maybe the pack needs to build better ties to the witch community of New York, after all.

Hell, maybe I need to spend a lot of long, serious days in financial meetings. The pack has money and maybe needs to meet with important financial advisors to invest it properly. Those would be in New York, right?

I could fly in, take the meetings, and then make my way down to her shop. It wouldn't be ideal, because the wolf hates the idea of not even being able to smell our mate while we hold her, but I'd take it. Whatever it takes.

"I'm sure something's coming up," I say, already turning over plans in my head.

"Where are you right now? At home?"

"Yeah. Celia hasn't sent me anywhere else yet."

"Where next?" she asks, and I think that's envy in her voice.

"No idea yet. Where would you go, if you could pick?"

"Everywhere," she sighs. It's unguarded and raw and leaves me completely blindsided. Not that Mae's never been unguarded and raw with me, because I have to believe she was, even in those few days we had. But there's a difference between being raw in bed and in a conversation.

I'd take her everywhere. I'd take her along with me to every place I travel to for pack business. I'd take her to see the world and relish every single moment we spend together doing it.

I pinch my thigh. That's a fantasy, and the reality is she's stuck in New York right now.

Maybe someday. I have to believe that. I have to, because if I let myself believe anything else, I'm worried I'll lose my mind.

Chapter Thirty-Two

Mae

The days fall into something of a routine.

Honestly, it's similar enough to how it was before Bryce entered my shop for the first time, with just a few additions. I still wake up at an ungodly hour, then suck down coffee laced with stimulant spells. I open the shop, and Violet comes in soon after. Now they're employed and are at the shop fifteen hours a week. They charge me for five more, insisting they're running down leads for people who need bigger spells, and I believe them, so I pay it.

We have a few customers here and there. It's mostly humans paying a few bucks for crystals, mostly unenchanted. I leave them to Violet, who still is obsessed with our crystal shelf. A few supernatural beings come in, looking for magical solutions to small problems. I sell a scrying orb, I enchant a siren's clothes to dry instantly on land, and I puzzle out an enchantment for a magical mouse trap guaranteed to really attract and catch the mice.

Honestly, in New York, that's not a bad line of products to consider marketing. I fiddle with the enchantment a bit when I have a spare minute. It's the type of actual, practical magic that I enjoy doing.

All of that is a pretty solid routine. Is it wildly enjoyable? No. Not even close. But it's tolerable, and I'll take tolerable.

I wasn't thrilled when Greta stuck me with her shop, but things weren't much better before that. It's always been about someday. Someday, I'd be able to do things. Go places. Find things I love.

Someday isn't here yet, but this isn't so bad.

There are only two additions to the routine, and both are going to drive me out of my mind.

The first is Clay. Just like Violet said, he comes to the door every single day. I've taken to hiding in the back most days when he comes by, because otherwise he just shouts at me to let him in.

And he never does come in, which I'm grateful for, but I cannot for the life of me figure out why not. He's smart enough to know the door isn't locked.

I have no idea what to do with him. I actually tried calling his mom, but she washed her hands of him years ago. I don't think he's listened to anyone since he was a teenager.

Greta, sometimes. Maybe if she was here, she could get through to him. But she's not here, and I just have to live with that.

The second change in routine is driving me out of my mind in an entirely different way. Bryce.

We've talked on the phone almost every night for the past two weeks. And it's not just him calling anymore, either. I initiate the calls about half the time, and I can't make myself stop.

I don't want to stop. Maybe I could have cut this off if I'd told him not to call me when we were still in the village. Maybe if I'd never let myself get to know him any better, I'd be able to resist him. But I doubt it.

He's been traveling to meet with some humans who want to clear-cut the forest around the village this past week, and I actually find myself eager to hear him grumble about his day with them. Because yes, he's as much of a grump as he promised me he is and complains about the humans and their antics every day. But he also talks about loving the natural beauty around his home and wanting to preserve it, and I can more than agree with that. That village was my first real taste of being somewhere else, and I'll always treasure that.

And he talks about his job with such passion. He's so dedicated to his pack, wanting to do everything he can for them. It's sweet, and humbling to hear, and so different from what I'm used to. I haven't seen my father in half a century and talk to my mother maybe four times a year. Witches have two extremes: we can either be incredibly territorial, or we're hands off. Most of the time, with a few special exceptions, we're hands off and disconnected. What's ours is ours, and we'll defend it to the death. But you have to be strategic about what you decide is yours, if you're going to be that extreme about it. And I've never known witches to truly build a community.

But here Bryce is, always grumbling about his day and more than happy to keep doing the job if it means taking care of his people.

Tonight he picks up on the third ring. "Sorry, getting out of the shower," he says, and I nearly groan at that. He's probably still naked. In a towel at most.

Gods, that's a nice thought. I'm tempted to ask him but refrain. That's not how this goes.

"Want me to call back?" I ask.

"No, I picked up dinner already, it's waiting for me—you have yours?" he asks, and I hear movement. Probably him getting his food.

"Yeah," I say, looking at the sandwich I pulled together. "How was your day?"

"Same old, same old," he says, and I hear a lid of something opening. "At least I'm done for now, though."

"Oh? Problem solved?" I ask. That's certainly not same old, same old, and I'm damn impressed. Humans love to cut down trees and destroy the world around them.

He snorts. "Not in the slightest. I'm sure I'll be back soon."

Oh. It makes sense, I guess, because Bryce is important and Celia probably has somewhere else she needs to send him.

From his stories, it always seems like he's off to somewhere. Hell, he was sent to find me, and I'm really not as significant as a group of well-funded humans with bulldozers. "Don't you ever get time off?" I ask him.

The question must seem out of nowhere, but he doesn't question it. That's another thing I like about him; he just rolls with whatever I'm thinking and never loses a step.

"I don't really have much use for time off," he says, and he actually sounds thoughtful, too, like the question wasn't random and invasive and instead something worth considering. "The pack is my life."

That sounds beautiful, in a way. But also very sad, and a little lonely.

What do I know about it? I've often been sad and lonely, and I don't even have a cause to dedicate my life to as a trade-off.

"Do you have anyone to help you?" I ask. "Anyone who can do what you do?"

He thinks about it for a minute, or maybe he's just eating his meal. I take his pause as an opportunity to get in a few bites of my own food. "There are a couple people. But a lot of the time, sending a Crae makes the difference, you know? When I show up there's no doubt that the full weight of the entire werewolf population is behind me. And that means something."

I suppose. It sounds like a lot to ask of anyone, though.

"What's for dinner tonight?" he asks me, seemingly tired of talking about his job.

It goes on like this, light questions. We talk about our food, and then he tells me about a human who demanded Bryce stay seated, intimidated by his size. I tell him about my mouse traps and Violet's new order of crystals that I don't even know how they snuck an order in for.

The food is gone. Night has long since fallen. "You going home in the morning?" I ask him when there's a lull in the conversation.

"Mhm. First thing."

"I should let you get to sleep then." I mean it, too—if he needs sleep, then I'll leave him be, and just be glad to have spoken to him at all.

But that's not how this goes, and we both know it.

"You want me to let you go?" he asks, because Bryce Crae is a good man, and he always checks.

"No." That's the last thing I want, actually.

I'm too reliant on this man. I want him too much. I should have given him up when I had the chance, because now I can't see myself doing it willingly. But I can't see a future where we work.

It's going to end in heartbreak, but for tonight, I don't have to think about that.

Tonight, it's going to end in an orgasm. It always does.

"Good," he says, voice dropping to a low rumble. "Get on your bed, Mae."

I do, untying the robe I put on after work and before I called him, letting it slide to the floor. I lie on my bed completely naked, knowing what his next question will be.

"What're you wearing for me today?" he asks, voice sending a delicious shiver up my spine.

This is usually the time where I tell him about whatever outfit I planned for the day, which he always listens to, asking for details until he breaks and tells me about how he wants to take it off. But not today. "Nothing."

"Nothing?"

"I'm naked for you. I couldn't wait," I tell him.

He groans, and I close my eyes, putting the phone on speaker before I do so I have my hands free. I palm my breast, spreading my thighs slightly, wondering what he looks like on the other end of the call.

"Good fucking girl," he growls.

"How about you?"

There's a sound like he's moving. "Nothing now. Had to catch up to you, little witch."

He can't have had that much on to be naked that quick. Maybe a towel, like I thought earlier, and I bite my lip, thinking of him sitting through our whole dinner in just a towel.

"Can you touch those beautiful tits for me?" he asks.

I bite back a moan. "Way ahead of you, there."

"Oh? Already ready to go tonight, Mae? Ready for me?" he teases.

"You ready for me?" I ask, circling my nipple.

"Now that I'm thinking about you touching your tits for me? Ready is an understatement," he admits.

I spread my thighs a little wider, a nearly automatic gesture, thinking of him ready between my legs.

I should be able to let this go. We only had sex a few times, after all. It's been weeks. There's so many things making this a bad idea—

"I haven't stopped thinking about how good your pretty cunt tasted," he says, interrupting and completely destroying my train of thought. "I dreamed about it last night."

My breath hitches. "Yeah?"

"Mhm. Touch it for me, little witch?"

I trail my free hand down my body, across my stomach, and down to my cunt, which is dripping and ready. Bryce's voice alone can do that now.

"What do I taste like?" I ask him, a slight hitch in my voice as I rub over my clit, my bucking hips almost sending the phone flying.

He groans. "Like fucking heaven, Mae. I'd do anything to taste it right now." Perhaps sensing that he's verging on the things we don't talk about, he quickly moves on. "You put your fingers inside you yet?"

"Not yet. You ready for me?"

"Since the moment I fucking heard your voice. What are you doing?"

"Got one hand on my nipple. The other on my clit."

I hear his breathing speed up, no doubt as he touches himself, getting closer. "Put a finger inside. Please."

I do, sliding one finger, then two, inside my cunt, using my thumb to keep stroking my clit.

Two fingers don't feel like enough. I like the stretch of a good cock, but I can't get off without touching my clit, so I usually skip putting something inside me when I rub one out. That was before I fucked Bryce. Now, I clench my inner muscles, wishing I was squeezing around his cock.

Gods, he knew exactly what to do with his cock—

My breath hitches and my hips roll against my own hand, seeking just that little more. "Bryce, I'm—"

"Close, little witch? Me too. Want to hear you come for me. Please."

And, like his asking is enough, I do.

I whimper and moan when I do, thrashing, trying to get more of my own damn hand, chasing something that isn't there.

"Oh, fuck, Mae, I—" A long groan comes across the call.

Bryce is breathing heavily when he's done. "Nothing has ever sounded more beautiful than you." He says things like that with such sincerity that it makes me want to actually believe him.

"That was really good," I say, lethargic and boneless on my bed, turning my head towards the phone languidly.

He manages a chuckle, although he sounds as worn out as I feel. "Yeah? I'm glad, Mae."

"So good," I confirm.

He's quiet for a moment, and we just breathe together. "Mae?" he says after a long minute.

"Yeah?"

"I won't be able to call for a day or two, alright? But, can I call you after that?"

I pause for a moment, thinking of what that could mean. He's traveling home tomorrow, but it's not that long a trip. And he's the one who started our calls in the first place.

But what can I say? *No, I feel irrationally like I'm being robbed of you, how dare you take yourself away from me?* Absolutely not.

He's not mine. Reality doesn't work that way.

"Please," I force myself to say. "Yeah, call me after that. I look forward to it." Then, not giving him time to say anything else, I say, "I should let you sleep. I know you have an early day tomorrow."

I don't give him a chance to interrupt and hang up the phone.

CHAPTER THIRTY-THREE

BRYCE

Today is going to be miserable. I know it from the second I wake up.

To be more accurate, I've known it for weeks. Since the minute she took Chase's hand and left me behind, really. But maybe I underestimated how miserable it would be, exactly.

I thought the last full moon, where all I could think about was Mae, was hard. I hadn't even smelled her yet. Hadn't touched her. The wolf is going to make me suffer this month.

I check out of the hotel right after the crack of dawn, just wanting to be home. A tight, desperate feeling coils in my gut the whole time, and I can't fight it. I want to call her. I stop myself from dialing a hundred times. But I know it won't help. What's it supposed to change?

She's not here. She's not at home. She's dealing with her own life, and that's the way it is.

If there was a way to knock a wolf unconscious for twelve hours or so, I'd gladly take it right about now.

I should ask Mae if there's some sort of spell—

I forcibly shake off the thought. I'm not surprised my brain turned immediately to Mae with no prompting, but I have to stop doing it. I have to let her go, at least for tonight, or I'm going to drive myself crazy.

The pack is busy when I arrive. No surprise; it's the full moon, after all. Everyone wants to make sure everything is done well before moonrise tonight.

Uncharacteristically, I ignore the pack. I don't check in with any of my siblings, not even Celia, not even to update her on what's going on with the humans. I go immediately to my house and immediately to my bedroom.

Mae's scent has almost completely faded from the room, but there's still the slightest trace of her on the sheets. A less sharp nose wouldn't notice it, but the wolf in me could scent even the smallest trace of her anywhere.

I have to hope that it will soothe the wolf tonight, and not just make things worse.

I have a simple plan for tonight: get rid of my clothes that smell like the hotel and other people and everything but Mae, curl up in bed, try to draw as much of her scent to me as I can, and don't move until long after the moon sets tomorrow.

I think it's a solid plan and I'm well on my way to starting it when Celia walks into my house.

"Ever knock?"

She leans against my bedroom door, arms crossed over her chest. "You left the door unlocked. And I didn't think you'd answer me."

"Got it in one."

"Yeah, well, you don't get to opt out of this one."

Half of me wants to bury my head in a pillow and ignore her, but I think we left off doing that when we were ten or so.

"What do you want, Celia?" I ask. I should get out of bed, talk this over in a more dignified way. A way that doesn't have me hiding under a sheet, face pressed against a pillow, watching my sister loom over me.

I can't quite make myself move.

"Are you going to be okay tonight?"

"It won't kill me," I say, and it won't. It's never killed a wolf to not have their mate on the full moon.

Being uncomfortable, hurt, made them a little crazy—now, all those things are possible. More than just possible, they're likely.

"Are you going to hurt yourself? Or try to run?"

I don't know. It's not like I have real full moon experience knowing she's my mate. I don't know what the wolf will drive me to do.

"Want to tie me down?" I ask her, mostly being facetious. But maybe it's not the worst idea. If the wolf tried to compel me to find her, who knows where I'd end up by the time the moon sets?

"Not particularly. And I don't think we have anything on hand for that." Her look could bore holes in me. "Callum volunteered to sit with you."

I wince, because that is the last thing I want.

For unmated wolves, the full moon brings out some more wolfish traits. Nothing unmanageable, usually. But for mated wolves...

Even with Mae not here, I'm still a mated wolf, and I won't be good company for Callum. And the last thing I want is for my brother to see me like that.

"I know," Celia says. "I told him. But he's worried you'll hurt yourself."

"I won't." I hesitate for a moment, but there's really nothing more embarrassing than Celia threatening to have our baby brother babysit me tonight, so I don't have much to lose. I reach into my pillow and pull out the lump I've been hiding there, my ripped button-down, worn by Mae and still carrying just enough of her scent. "I'll be okay."

Her eyes soften when she sees the shirt. "Take care of yourself," she says, and then turns to walk away.

Celia's never been one for wasting words, and I appreciate it.

The shirt now out in the open, I bring it to my face, inhale deeply, and try to close my eyes.

***

That night is hell.

It drags on for what feels like centuries. The closest approximation I can make is a night centuries ago, where I laid awake after being poisoned, body tormented just to the point of agony, but my healing kicking in before I could pass out.

I grip that damned shirt like it's a lifeline, like it's going to save me from this. It's not even her shirt, and she only wore it for an hour or so. The scent barely clings to it.

It doesn't matter. I'd sooner give up my arm than give up that shirt.

I want to go to her, to hold her, please her, and the wolf inside me can't understand why I'm not doing those things. I'm a mated wolf; I should be at her side. Always, but especially tonight. There should be no exception to that rule.

When the moon finally sets and releases its hold on me, I'm a sweaty, anxious mess, still curled up around an old shirt in bed, and I finally pass out.

Chapter Thirty-Four

Mae

"Mae?" Violet calls from the front.

I sigh, looking away from my enchantment. I'm doing a batch of the stimulant spells, trying to see if they're marketable to anyone as addicted as me, but Violet's interruption breaks my concentration.

I look at the clock. It's about time for Clay to come by again. Has he done something stupid? Escalated somehow?

Well, I won't leave poor Violet to deal with my deranged cousin, so I walk into the main room of the shop, intent on helping them out.

Clay isn't there. Instead, there's a good-looking demon leaning against a display shelf, surveying the room. It takes me a moment to place him.

Chase. Bryce's brother-by-fate.

"Is he okay?" I blurt out. Is Bryce okay? What could have happened that would have brought this demon to my door?

Or maybe the spell failed again, and they decided I was too much of a liability for Bryce to handle, knowing he'd be soft on me, and sent Chase instead.

"He's alive," Chase says, interrupting my thoughts.

"Alive isn't okay."

"No, it's not. Any idea what last night was?"

"He didn't call me last night. He told me he wouldn't." Something like fear grips me. Something has happened, and I have no idea what it is.

"Yeah, he tell you why?" I shake my head. "Seen a lunar calendar recently, Mae?"

Lunar calendar. My stomach drops.

"Is he okay?" I repeat. I have no idea what the full moon actually does to werewolves. I didn't ask. But Chase's intense stare is telling me it's serious.

He just looks at me for a long moment and then sighs. "I haven't actually seen him yet, but Heath and Callum went by this morning and said he looked like shit."

I try not to feel guilty. I didn't ask him to develop this crazy mating bond. I didn't ask for this at all.

I can only mostly squash the guilt.

"So I thought, you know what, you should know what's going on," he continues. "So I popped over here to tell you." He gives me a long look. "You didn't even know this could happen, did you?"

I shake my head, and something about his expression softens. He sighs, and some of the tension in his body fades away. "I was prepared for the mating bond. Wolves are a little different than demons, but I could figure it out. I knew what Heath and I would need from each other. Bethany and Celia were obviously prepared. We should have anticipated this. Should have supported you."

"I was in your village for a day," I point out dryly. "We didn't have time to have these conversations."

"I could have come here. I should have. Then maybe I wouldn't be dragging my ass here the day after a full moon when I should be in bed."

"Sorry."

"Well, I'm here now."

I nod. "He's going to be okay?"

"You sound like you care."

"I do care. Just because I have a life here that I can't just quit on doesn't mean I don't care about him." I care about him way, way more than I ever should.

Not getting a call from him last night genuinely ruined my night.

But apparently not as much as I ruined his.

I take a deep breath. "What exactly happens on the full moon?"

"You sure you want all those details? It's pretty graphic, and from what I remember—"

"I'll throw you straight out of my shop and call Bryce," I threaten. "He'll answer any question I ask him." Even if he probably doesn't want to. Even if it might embarrass him, if he really did look like shit this morning, and had avoided telling me why last night was special.

"You already figured that much out, huh?"

I take a deep, deep breath, forcing myself to keep my cool. "Violet," I say, suddenly remembering my assistant who called me out here in the first place. "Why don't you take your lunch?"

"I took lunch an hour ago."

"Listen, I don't care what you call it then, but—"

They roll their eyes. "I'll give you an hour."

I wait until they leave and the door swings shut behind them, then turn my full attention back to Chase. "Alright, you have my attention. What happened?"

He looks at me for a long moment. "Wolves fuck on the full moon," he says bluntly. "Not to put too fine a point on it. Mated wolves fuck like it's going out of style. Basically a compulsion."

Oh. That's... something.

My mind gets caught on the unfortunate implications of what so many of the wolves I met got up to last night. No wonder Chase is making snide comments about how he should be in bed right now.

And then I process the bigger picture. "And Bryce?" I ask. Did he fuck someone else? I can't really blame him if he did. I have no hold on him, not really.

The idea makes my blood boil, though. Makes me want to plant a claim on him, plant a flag, tell all the other wolves to back the fuck off.

"He suffered," Chase says bluntly. "From what I understand it's pretty agonizing. The wolf inside them is pushing for their mate and doesn't really understand why their mate isn't there."

That sounds awful. "Will he be okay?"

"Blue balls never killed a guy, despite what they'll tell you," he quips.

Blue balls. So he didn't fuck someone else.

No, instead he just suffered. "What do I do for him?"

I worry he's going to say go to him. But I can't. I can't leave this place, everything Greta asked me to do. It would be irresponsible, and a poor way to pay Greta back for everything she did for me.

He shrugs. "Fuck if I know."

"Do you have anything useful to tell me?" I snap.

"Not really. But I thought you should know. Since he's your mate and all."

"Witches don't have mates."

He snorts. "Puh-lease. You're obsessed with him."

"I have eyes. They work."

"I just bet they do."

"Look, just because he's the best fuck I've had in a while doesn't mean I'm ready to change my life over him."

"Alright, witch. I get it." Then he gets serious. "Look, I don't want to think about how Bryce is in bed, okay, that's so far from my business and he's like my brother. But you're taking phone sex from the guy. If all you wanted was to get laid, you'd move on, right?"

I bite my lip, because he is absolutely right. And I don't know what to say about it.

He shrugs. "Just something to think about. Anyways, I thought you should know. I'll leave you in peace."

And before I can argue or say anything, or ask anything else, Chase disappears.

CHAPTER THIRTY-FIVE

MAE

B ryce does a good job at hiding how hard the full moon was on him over the phone.

He doesn't even mention the full moon. He acts like it never happened, like that particular day means no more to him than any other.

He gets suspicious of me tiptoeing around it, though. I don't want to ask, not if he's not going to bring it up first. I'm not sure if it's my place, given everything.

"Everything all right?" he asks. Like something's wrong with me, like I'm the one to worry about here.

"Fine," I promise him. "Everything's fine."

I don't think he believes me, but he lets it go.

***

He's back on the road two days later, and I worry that's not enough time to recover from whatever the full moon did to him. But what the hell do I know? Maybe he needs a distraction.

"Humans, again?" I ask, sitting and painting my nails while I listen to him move around his room, re-packing his bag.

"Sirens," he tells me. "We have trade agreements to hammer out." His voice gets muffled for a moment as he steps further away from the phone, probably going to the closet, but then he comes back. "What're you up to?"

Clay stood at the door for almost an hour today. I don't mention it. "You know," I say, capping the polish and admiring my nails. "Same old same old."

***

A week after the full moon, Chase shows back up.

I'm working the counter this time, although it's not like we have any customers who need someone at the register. We had a customer this morning, a human who was looking for something to help with a bad relationship. I let Violet deal with them.

"We have a door," I tell him.

"Demons don't need doors. Right?" he says to Violet.

They look at him. "Polite demons use doors."

He grins. "I'm not polite. So it's fine. You half demon?"

They nod. "Half demon, half witch."

"That must be interesting magic."

They give him a sharp smile. "You have no idea." They turn to me. "I'm going to bring the deliveries around."

Chase looks at me when they leave. "Deliveries?"

"Violet's good at this," I admit, propping my elbows on the counter. "They've got a good two dozen clients on, like, subscription services now. Stimulant spells, enchanted crystals that don't last forever, even a few enchantments mean to protect the home or keep kitchens clean or whatever. It's actually making money."

I shouldn't sound so impressed. Mostly I'm just a little pissed I never thought of it. How many times did I throw ideas around, but never follow through?

Violet got hired and took action. They might be the difference between this place going under and surviving.

Greta should have left the store to them.

"Good. I'm glad. Bryce said you guys were struggling here."

I duck my head at that to hide the blush that's probably covering my face. Oh, he's spreading that around, is he?

I suppose it probably wasn't that good a secret in the first place. But I don't love that they all know that I can't keep my shop in order.

"Hey, no shame in it," Chase says, clearly seeing my reaction. "I've never tried to run a business but I hear it's hard as hell."

"Yeah," I agree. "I don't know what Greta was thinking."

"She probably thought you could handle it."

Then she was wrong, I think but don't say. I don't want to handle this.

The store won't close this month. Violet and I will both get paid. We're not really making a significant profit, but we're not totally in the red anymore, either. With the work I did for the werewolves, I've paid off Greta's debts—that I know about—and can invest in some good quality merchandise. It should feel like a victory.

"What are you doing here?" I ask to change the subject.

He hesitates a second, but then admits, "A few reasons. The first is that Heath asked me to come."

"Oh?"

"Sister-by-fate, pack bonds, all of that. Whether or not you choose Bryce, you're permanently going to be part of their pack now, so you should get used to it. And he wanted to make sure you were alright."

"And the other reasons?"

"I dumped the full moon thing on you and ran last time. I thought you might have questions. And besides, I don't get to hang out with many casters. It's an interesting change of pace."

"No demon friends?"

His eyes grow darker, just for a moment, like a cloud passes over them. "I have a brother, but I didn't leave Demonheim in the best circumstances. Things are different, there."

That seems like a minefield I don't want to touch. But all I need to know is he spends all his time with the wolves, and he could probably use some contact with casters.

"I have no idea how your magic works," I tell him. "I know it's different from mine and it's probably different from Violet's. But if you're up for it, join me in the back. We can be casters together."

***

He comes three times a week, right around when Violet goes out to do deliveries, and stays for an hour or so every time. He's not bad company, all things considered.

He tells me things about the village, things Bryce never got around to telling me. Old friendships, and celebrations, and everyone's favorite places and things.

"I've known Bryce four hundred years, about," he says, shrugging when he tells me a particularly hilarious story about a bad case of poison ivy that lasted almost eight hours before Bryce's healing managed to resolve it. It's the kind of story that Bryce would never tell me himself, but Chase's description of Bryce's snarling, grumpy reaction to realizing he fell asleep in a pile of poison ivy makes me laugh, anyway.

"Four hundred years?" I sputter.

"Oh right, I forgot. You're an itty-bitty baby," he teases.

"And you're an old-ass man."

"True, true. But some things get better with age. As I imagine you recently discovered."

He is not wrong about that. But I'm not going to admit it, not to him.

He knows anyway though, and smirks.

I don't have to come up with a retort, because there's a furious banging on the door. "Did Violet lock it when they left?" Chase asks, but I don't respond. I know who it is.

"Mae, don't be a bitch!"

Chase winces. "Who the fuck is talking to you like that?"

I walk to the front of the shop. "Go the fuck away, Clay. Take a fucking hint and leave."

His face is twisted in a mask of fury, and he bangs on the door again. "Don't be such a fucking bitch."

He sounds wrong. Deranged, really. Worse than he's sounded any other time he's come by, and even with the glass between us, I can see something around his eyes. Something so far beyond angry or unsettled. It sets something off inside me, putting me instantly on the defensive.

Clay looks bad. His usually handsome, smooth-talking features are mottled with rage, but even his clothes look worse, like they don't quite fit him anymore. I gape at him, watching how far my cousin has fallen.

Chase is behind me in an instant. "I can kill him for you," he offers, almost casually. "Jealous ex?"

"My cousin."

"And what does he want?"

"This shop."

"And I thought you were practically ready to give the thing away."

"Not to him."

"Got it." Chase disappears and reappears outside, behind Clay. I watch him sway a bit as he lands, and know from everything he's told me about his magic that he's dipped into his own energy supply to do that. Show-off.

"She said get lost," he says, almost conversational, but it doesn't take a genius to see the menacing way he looms over Clay.

"Who're you? Her guard dog?"

Chase leans in, and suddenly, I see him for what he is in a way I never have before. A demon, from the pits of Demonheim, ready to torture and absolutely remorseless about it.

"I'm the guy who's going to fuck you up if you bother her again."

"This isn't your business." Clay tries to pull himself taller, and on anyone else, it would work. But Chase makes him look small.

"I will put you in Demonheim myself if you don't get lost right now," Chase says, his voice menacingly, bitingly level as he says it.

Clay seems to evaluate his options for a long, long moment before he turns back to me. "I'll be back, Mae." And then he walks off.

I watch him go, unable to take my eyes off the scene. Is it just my imagination, or is he limping?

Chase comes back inside, this time using the door like a normal person. "Your cousin?" he snaps, the stony mask from a minute ago shattered.

I wave a hand, aiming for nonchalant and knowing I fail by a mile. "Behold, the reason Greta was so insistent I take this place. So Clay didn't get it."

"Yeah, I can fucking see why. He come by a lot?"

"Most days." Every day, now.

"But he doesn't come in?" His eyes are intense. "He hasn't laid a hand on you, has he?"

I shake my head.

Chase takes a deep breath, like he's steadying himself. He looks at his watch, a big, clunky thing I'd tease him for being an old man item if the mood wasn't so tense. "Heath can wait," he decides. "What kind of defensive enchantments can you set up?"

CHAPTER THIRTY-SIX

BRYCE

"Why didn't you tell me about your cousin?" I ask her over the phone.

She goes silent for a minute. I wish I could see her. I wish I could smell her. Instead, I have to wait for her to say it.

And she didn't tell me about the belligerent cousin calling her a bitch outside her home nearly every day.

"What would you have done?" she asks after a moment.

"Parked my ass at your door and taught him a thing or two," I say immediately. What would I have done? I'd have defended my damn mate, that's what. And that should never have been in question.

"Don't be ridiculous. You have work."

"You're ridiculous if you think I care more about meeting nymphs than I do about you."

She's silent again, and it twists my heart. "You love your job."

"You matter more," I say back with absolutely no hesitation. Something I've never said before. I have never had something to place above my job.

With Mae, though, there's no question.

She's quiet again. I'm half-tempted to say fuck the nymphs, walk out of the meetings scheduled for tomorrow, and fly to New York, just to actually see her during these damn pauses, get a read on her.

"I'm taking care of it," she says eventually. "He's my cousin, and he's an ass and he lost everyone's support decades ago, but something's wrong with him. I'm handling it. You should have seen some of the things Chase, Violet, and I came up with."

The only reason I'm not already in New York is because Chase told me about those things. Apparently, Violet and Mae are quite creative when it comes to protecting themselves and the shop.

Good. I'm glad my mate can look after herself, although I wish I was there. And maybe it's the wolf in me, because I know her magic is powerful and will protect her, but I wish there was something physical like my claws and teeth between her and danger.

"You'll call me, or Chase, if he's a problem, right?" I press.

She sighs, and I don't need to see her in person to interpret that one. "Yeah. I promise."

"Good." Time to move on; I don't want her to have to think about that asshole more than necessary. "How's business been? Yesterday you said Violet was looking at some new clients?"

"I think Violet scored our rent for the month," she says.

"That's good." She's always so worried about the shop, a shop it barely seems like she wants, and if Violet is taking some of that load off her shoulders, then I'll be eternally thankful to the other witch.

"Yeah," she agrees, but she sounds distracted as she says it. "Violet is way, way better at this than I ever was."

I almost remind her that, by all accounts, Violet seems to want this when Mae doesn't. But I don't think she'd take kindly to me reminding her that the shop she's dedicated everything to isn't something she even wants. Instead, I tell her, "You've been doing wonderful things for the shop. You've told me all about them."

She's silent for a moment. "Nothing that great."

"The magic you're doing sounds damn impressive, and like you're creating things people actually need. Just because it's not like what Greta did or what Violet thinks of doesn't mean it isn't great, Mae. You're impressive."

She says nothing again, but I hear a slight hitch in her breathing on the other side.

People don't tell my mate how wonderful she is often enough. But I'll fix that now. She'll hear it every day.

She is impressive, and I love hearing about her accomplishments. Do I wish she was happier with them? Of course. But if she's set on doing this, on running this shop for her cousin, then I'll make sure she recognizes all her successes along the way.

"I'm thinking of coming to New York in a few weeks," I tell her. Maybe after the next full moon, judging by my schedule. I'm sure I'll be absolutely desperate to see her by then. "Would that be okay with you?"

"I don't own the city," she says, instantly. Not the answer I want to hear, and I think of how to respond to that, before she says, much quieter, "And I'd like to see you. Please. Come here. I know you don't like the shop, but please, come see me."

My heart fills with so much warmth just hearing it. "It'd be my pleasure, little witch," I manage to tell her, already thinking about it.

***

"No, I don't have anywhere for you to go," Celia tells me, sitting at her kitchen table and giving me an unimpressed look. "Go home."

"There must be something." I begin to pace the space.

"Go home," my sister tells me. "Have you seen yourself? Take a nap."

I don't tell her it's hard to sleep. That at first, it was easier if I went to sleep right after hanging up the phone with Mae. But it's not working anymore. We're approaching another full moon and I already feel the dread of her absence, even with days to prepare. I don't tell her that my home feels empty and cold without Mae.

She spent one night in my bed, and I'll never recover.

And I'd never want to recover. She's my mate, fills every inch of my soul, and I've longed for her since I was old enough to know what it meant to want. I've waited for her, and I've been blessed to find her.

And I just want to have her. To know she's at home, or to go wherever she is. To hold her and kiss her, and watch whatever stunning outfit she puts on for the day. To watch her drink her coffee and tell her how wonderful she is. To smell what I do to her, and then take care of her exactly like we both need.

But I can't have any of that, so I need a distraction. The distraction Celia is denying me.

Bethany sets a plate of food down. "Eat before you collapse," she tells me.

If Bethany and Celia are saying it, then I really must look like shit. I sit.

"You need to go to her, Bryce," Bethany says, sitting down at the table next to Celia.

"I am. I booked a ticket. Next week."

She shakes her head. "I don't mean to visit."

My breath catches. "What're you saying, Bethany?"

"Exactly what you think she is," Celia picks up for her mate. "She's your mate, Bryce. If she needs to be there, then you need to be with her, not fucking around here looking for stupid distractions."

I swallow. "I have a duty to this pack," I manage to say. I've always had a duty to this pack. I've always put the pack first.

"You have a duty to your mate," Bethany insists, voice quiet but very firm.

Celia nods. "I'd still expect you to do some of your duty, just from there. And Bryce, as good as you are, maybe it's time to admit there are plenty of people you can delegate to. You don't have to do it all. You have a mate now. Focus on her first."

"It might not be forever," Bethany continues. "She needs to be there right now, but who's to say that's still true in ten years?"

"Plus, between Chase and the invention of the airplane, it's not like we won't see you, or you won't be able to get to pack business."

They planned this, I realize dimly, this rehearsed tag-team in front of me a carefully orchestrated dance. I must really look like shit, if they're resorting to this.

The thing is, it sounds so good. I want to get on the plane right now, change my ticket, and take Mae in my arms. Say fuck it all, fuck everything but her.

But I've always put this pack first. I can't leave it all behind. Celia took the throne, and I did what I could to alleviate that burden. I did my part, always.

Can I just quit that? Leave it to Celia to figure out how to replace me?

"Think about it," Bethany says, always the more gentle of the two. "When you visit her, think about if you could live there with her, alright?"

I nod, my mind spinning.

CHAPTER THIRTY-SEVEN

MAE

Violet brings home a contract that will easily pay the rent, and I just stare at it.

"How'd you do this?" I ask them, absolutely dumbfounded as I read the hand-written agreement over and over again.

They shrug. "I mean, I can't do it alone. This isn't all my type of magic."

I look it over, and they're right, at least a little. Most of it is things Violet could handle, but they've left room for me here, too.

"What do you think?" They ask after I spend a long, long minute looking it over.

I look up at them, fidgeting in front of me. They look so young. Are so young, even younger than me, barely an adult. They're nervous, hands wringing together while they wait, and all I can think is that they're already a hundred times better at this than I am.

"I think I need to get you a raise," I manage to tell them, and they smile bashfully.

"I'm going to do the jewelry," they say, turning away to go into the back, and I watch them go, thinking.

***

It shouldn't hurt, because I never wanted to be good at this, but it takes me a while to get over it.

I feel like I've failed Greta, is the thing, and that's the one thing I never wanted to do.

My rather mediocre magic disappointing both my parents was something I could brush off. More skilled witches like Cesily and Clay look down on me and my simple spells and human jobs, and I let their judgment slide right off my back. But Greta I wanted to impress. I wanted to live up to the care she'd shown me.

She's only ever asked one thing of me. And I can't do it. I don't want to do it.

When Bryce calls that night, I don't talk about Violet and the new contract and the money and the shop. I ask him about his day and he tells me he's in the village, and that he went for a long walk through the woods today. He sounds disgruntled, like he can't imagine that's what he did with his time.

It sounds wonderful. And all I can think is, I want to be there too. With him, walking in the woods. And I can't squash the thought.

***

The next time Chase shows up, he looks uncharacteristically awkward. "I have a favor to ask you."

I look over my messy work table. "If it's enchanted jewelry, ask Violet. Mouse traps I can do, though."

"No, it's—" He sounds serious, so I turn my full attention to him. "We're a day away from the full moon. And I'm worried about Bryce."

I'm worried about him too, honestly. And I've been thinking more and more about what that might mean.

"He'd kill me for telling you this, but Heath told me that, last full moon, Bryce had a shirt? That you wore? It still smelled like you."

I flush a bit, because I know exactly what shirt he means. The button-down I'd taken from Bryce after we made the spell work in the woods, after we fucked against a tree. I just bet it smelled like me.

"I was hoping I could have some of your clothes, or sheets, or whatever. Something to help him get through it."

The idea is so unappealing I can't even think about it. Give Bryce my laundry and leave him to suffer?

No. I can't do this anymore. I've known for days now. Probably longer. And thinking about Bryce suffering? That's the final straw.

"Counter-offer," I say. "Is it true that demons are good at contracts, or is that just a stereotype?"

He looks at me for a long moment, and I think he has an idea of what I'm about to do. "A stereotype can be true," he says slowly. "What do you have in mind?"

***

In the end, Chase and I write a document that divides ownership of the shop into thirds. A third left for Greta, because maybe she'll show back up one day. I can hope. A third for me, because she wanted me to have it, so I won't abandon it entirely. And a third for Violet, who probably deserves it more than either of us, at this point.

"I'm not actually a lawyer, you know," Chase says about an hour in, but he seems to be doing a good job at working through all the details anyway.

"Could've fooled me."

"Demons are just good at finding loopholes. That's how our magic works, essentially. And you've asked me to do the exact opposite. You've asked me to close loopholes."

"And you're so good at it."

He flips me off instead of responding, reading the document in front of him again. "I think this is as good as it's going to get," he says, setting it on the table before he looks at me. "Does this mean what I think it means?"

"I'm coming back with you," I confirm. "I just need to pack. And tell Violet, I guess."

He doesn't say anything, but I think his smile says it all.

I feel lighter just for having said it. For having put it into the world. I'm not giving up on the shop, not really. I'm just doing it differently than Greta intended.

And it's not like Violet is a bad person to leave it with. The shop is safer in their hands than it ever was in mine.

I feel like I could fly. I feel some sort of power sparking at my fingertips, not entirely dissimilar to the power I felt that night in the woods.

This is the right choice, and I know it. All that's left to do is tell Violet.

***

Violet reads the entire document four times before they even look at me.

I'm already standing by with two packed bags and ready to go. I packed nearly everything I'd consider important enough to need right away, figuring I can send for everything else later. I'm dressed too, and made up, spending perhaps more time thinking of how I'd like Bryce to see me again than I did packing. And after all that, I realize with a sinking feeling that I never even considered what I'd do if Violet rejected this.

Violet wanted to work here so badly, and I just assumed they'd take this offer gladly. But what do I do if they don't?

Finally, they look up. "This is a big change," they say.

"You deserve it. And I won't be here, but I'll come back. I'm not abandoning you. I'll still do my part."

Violet gives me a shaky smile. "I'm happy for you. You should go."

If it were anyone else, I'd think I was getting kicked out the door. But Violet's smile is heart-meltingly sincere. "Call if you need me, okay?"

They nod. "Wait, before you go." They turn to the crystal shelf, and I chuckle. Of course. How could I have ever expected anything else?

They hand me a necklace with a white stone polished to a shine hanging on the charm. It's carved like a moon, and I think it might be moonstone.

It doesn't feel enchanted in any way, but I take it from them anyway with nearly reverent fingers. From Violet, it means something, enchantment or no enchantment.

"For your new start," they say, and their eyes are so sincere that I can't help myself, clasping the necklace on before giving them a hug.

They let go first. "You have places to be," they say, and grab a pen off the counter. "So let's sign this."

We do, and when it's all official, Chase takes my hand and whisks me away.

***

He brings me and my bags to the front step of Bryce's home, and I'm left a little woozy from the energy toll of traveling so far.

"You're not going to fall over, are you?" he asks, looking me over. "Because I really don't want to see what Bryce would be like if the first time he sees his mate in weeks is with her unconscious in my arms."

"No I am not going to fall over, I'm—" fine, I was going to say, but I can't finish because the door flies open.

Bryce looks nearly feral. He's not even dressed for the day, his shirt missing and his pants looking slept in. His hair is a mess, he has significant stubble on his face, and his eyes are beyond wild.

Those eyes latch on me almost immediately, and he freezes, as if he can't believe what he sees.

Chase backs away, leaving us to it. Probably smart, all things considered.

"Mae?" Bryce asks.

I step into his space and pull him down for a kiss. He returns it enthusiastically, almost viciously, grabbing at my waist and tugging me closer, biting at my lip.

His hands clasp my waist, then move over my back, like he has to touch every inch of me immediately, like he needs to prove I'm real.

I break the kiss, and it's clearly sooner than he'd like, because he dips his head forward, looking for more. I turn my head. "Invite me in?" I ask.

He stares at me for a long moment, then a rumbling starts in his chest. "I don't have to invite you anywhere. This is your damn house too," he says, and then he physically picks me up and carries me inside.

CHAPTER THIRTY-EIGHT

BRYCE

Mae. Here, in my home. Our home. In my arms, legs tight around my waist, letting me carry her to the couch. My hands tighten on her thighs convulsively, and I know I need to get a hold of it, need to make myself be gentle.

Celia's refusal to give me a new job and the upcoming full moon has driven me to the edge, and I'm not my best self right now. I look like some sort of frightening monster, I'm sure, and I need to continuously remind myself to be gentle with her.

What does it say that I can't be gentle with my mate? That I'm so close to the edge that I'm holding and squeezing her and not able to control it? That one sniff of her scent in the air sent me into what I might honestly call a frenzy, barreling down the stairs to the door to prove that she was real?

She's not complaining, though. Far from it. Her legs are fully locked around my waist, and it's a good thing I've lived in this house, with this layout, for almost a century now, because her hands are in my hair, holding me to her, not allowing me to break the kiss so I can navigate where we're going.

I fall onto the couch with her on my lap and hold her close to me. "Why're you here?" I ask, face buried in her neck as soon as she breaks the kiss, kissing and sucking the skin there, letting my mind fill with her scent.

Gods, her scent. I've missed it so much, been desperate for it. I want to drown in it, want it to fill my pores, our home. Never want to lose the smell of her again.

She moans lightly, tipping her head to give me more access to her neck. Her fingers are still in my hair, like she has to hold me. Like I'd let anything in the world drag me away from her.

"The full moon is tomorrow," she says.

I'm well aware, and it still doesn't explain why she's here, but I'm too busy being desperate for her to push for a better answer.

Let her keep her secrets. I have her.

"Let me take you upstairs," I practically beg, peppering her neck with kisses while I wait for her to give me permission.

She sighs and tightens her hold in my hair. "Yes. Please, Bryce."

I stand, hands cupping her back and ass to hold her to me, and make my way upstairs. "I want you so bad," I tell her, mostly in warning. But in case she doesn't get it, I add, "I'm not sure how gentle I can be."

She laughs breathlessly and tightens her legs around me. "Let's do it, then."

I reach the top step and slam her against the wall, using my hands to make sure she doesn't hit her head. "Little witch," I growl, face once more buried in her neck, "I'm going to fuck you senseless."

And then I pull back enough to rip through the damned shirt keeping us apart.

She looks down at the tatters of fabric. "I thought you liked this one." She says it so mildly, like she's not really invested either way.

It's the same top she wore the day I learned she was my mate. The see-through one that clings to every curve and teasingly hides her nipples and nothing else. I love that shirt.

I love her tits more, though, and feast my eyes hungrily on them. "I'll buy you a hundred of them," I tell her absently, hoisting her higher so her tits are at eye level, so I can lean in and nuzzle my face there. "But right now, I don't give a fuck how hot your clothes are. Just want you."

She shivers. "That stubble..."

"Don't like it?"

She moans, and I pull back to see I've left her skin red. But with her healing, it's already fading, and she doesn't complain, just shivers again under the weight of my gaze.

I suck one nipple into my mouth, biting lightly just to hear her moan for me again. I run my tongue over it, soothing the bite, and Mae grips my head so hard her nails must leave little indents on my scalp.

"I thought you said you were going to fuck me." Her tone is demanding, and something in me rebels at that. Not because I don't like her demanding—I think I'd do just about anything she told me to right now—but because it sounds too put-together.

And I can't have that. I can't have this night ending with her anything less than a fucked-out mess. Completely, absolutely reminded that she likes being here, being in my bed. I need to motivate her to stick around.

So I move, gripping her tight as I carry her into my bedroom, dropping her onto the bed. I want to pounce on her, to overwhelm her with pleasure. But I'm enraptured and can't help taking a minute to watch her.

My little witch. Absolutely, completely captivating.

Then she wiggles her hips, trying to take down her skirt without getting up.

I move to the boots she's still wearing, finding the zippers on the sides and pulling them down. There must be three inches of heel on these things, and I marvel she can walk in them at all.

"No fishnets today?" I ask her, dropping the boots and grabbing at her skirt, tugging it down, eyes caressing her legs as I go. It's the same leather miniskirt she wore that first day. The same bodysuit I've now destroyed.

She wiggles, pushing the skirt past her fantastic ass. "I wanted to make it as easy for you to get to me as possible."

That lights something up inside me, possession sparking in my ribcage, a pleased grumble from the wolf. My mate. Wanting me. Planning on how to get me into bed.

I toss the skirt to the floor, then pull the scraps of the bodysuit away from her. "Did you come here to get fucked, little witch?" I growl, looking her over, eyes hungrily drinking in every naked inch of her.

She's perfect like this, beautiful tits and belly and warm, inviting cunt on display, thighs spreading slightly under my gaze. I look up to her face, still thinking about how she planned this, when her lips curl into a smirk that makes me want to howl.

"I came for so much more than that, big guy—but we could start with the fucking?"

I have to decide between asking her what she means and fucking her immediately. It's no contest.

CHAPTER THIRTY-NINE

MAE

The intensity in his eyes makes my thighs clench.

He looks like he wants to eat me, devour me whole. Like his every thought is consumed fully with me, like he hasn't thought of a single other thing in our time apart.

He looks like he's going to fuck me hard and deep and so, so thorough.

And this is the day before the full moon. If everything Chase told me about full moons is true, then I can't even imagine what Bryce will be like tomorrow night.

I spread my thighs, just a bit. Just trying to show him I'm ready. That I'm here for this.

He thinks I'm only here to get fucked, apparently, but I don't think I can dissuade him of that until I let him fuck this desperation out of his system. And it won't exactly be a chore for me, either.

I crook a finger. "C'mon and fuck me like you promised."

He growls and falls on the bed, legs bracketing mine, pants rubbing against my naked skin. I shiver, reaching for him, but my hands fall and curl in the sheets when he shoves two fingers into my cunt.

"Already fucking wet," he growls. "For me?"

He sounds almost desperate to know.

I try to ride his fingers, try to push down on them, but he uses his other hand to pin my hips. He curls his fingers inside me and I thrash, but he holds me tight and I can't move. "For you," I confirm, breathless, chest heaving. "Now give me more."

His thumb finds my clit, making me moan and my back arch again, but that's not what I meant by more. I want him inside me. I want this powerful, practically feral man to fuck me like he means it.

"C'mon, Bryce. I need you in me. Now."

He growls, giving a particularly hard thrust of his fingers, but then withdraws them. "Whatever my mate wants," he murmurs, pushing his pants down his thighs, freeing his cock.

I bite my lip, watching it, watching a bead of pre-come at the tip. That's going to be inside me.

I clench at the thought, waiting for it, desperate for it.

He grabs my hips and lifts me so my ass is off the bed, legs wrapped around his waist. And then he pushes into me, one long, even push that has me grabbing at the sheets, desperate for something to hold on to as my head falls back and my eyes close.

Good gods, I didn't think I could possibly ever forget a single detail about my time with Bryce, but somehow I must have gotten a little fuzzy on how big he is. Every inch of me is filled and stretched, and it's so overwhelming and so, so good.

"Okay, Mae?" he asks, completely stopping, and somewhere in me it occurs to find that sweet, that even as practically feral as he's been, he still stops to check in.

I squeeze my legs around him tighter. "Fuck me like you mean it, Bryce," I tell him, and prepare to hold on for the ride of my life.

I get it, too, with Bryce growling and starting an excruciatingly delicious rhythm. Every time he pushes fully back inside me has me seeing stars, and within a moment, I can't control my moans. I give up, giving him exactly what we both wanted tonight, letting my head fall back and my eyes close, my hands squeezing the sheets as he fucks me senseless.

"Yes, Bryce, oh—that's it, that's it—" I'm babbling between moans, I know I am, but I can't stop it.

He can't either, continuous streams of my name and mate and little witch pouring from him, the reverent sound of his voice complimenting the brutal, claiming movement of his hips.

He drives me higher and higher, pushing me closer to that edge, until at last his thumb finds my clit again and he growls, "Come, little witch," and I'm helpless to do anything else, back bowing off the bed, legs squeezing him closer as pleasure wracks my body.

That seems to be what he was waiting for, because he roars my name as he comes too, thrusts becoming erratic and punishing, hand still on my hip squeezing tight enough to possibly bruise as he comes inside me.

When I feel like I have any control at all over my muscles again, I smile up at him, removing my hands from the sheets so I can reach for him.

He catches my hand in mid-air and brings it to his mouth, keeping eye contact with me as he kisses every fingertip, a slow, sensuous move that makes me wonder if he thinks I'm up for going again tonight.

"Did I hurt you?" he murmurs, at last returning my hand to me. He then trails his hands down to my legs, stroking skin as he moves, and gently untangles my legs from his hips.

I sprawl out on the bed, wide open and leaking come and very much sore and so, so satisfied. "In the best way," I tell him.

"I'm sorry. The wolf—"

"The wolf can do that to me again, believe me," I tell him. "Maybe not every time—" Gods, my cunt would never recover if he pounded me that hard every time—"But trust me, it can happen again."

He looks at me for a long moment, like he's worried I'm lying. But he must see my sincerity, because he nods. "Let me clean you up," he says, and gets off the bed, much to my displeasure.

He returns with a washcloth and a glass of water, offering me the glass while he gently cleans the come from my thighs and cunt.

The washcloth gets tossed away, presumably to wherever my skirt and shoes went. The top is a lost cause, I remember hazily. He tore it to get at my tits.

And that's honestly attractive enough that I won't complain about the loss of the bodysuit.

"Can I hold you?" I ask him, because he's hovering nervously now, and I need him to know we're okay. I need him here and with me so we can talk.

Bryce takes the invitation and in less time than it takes me to blink, I have him half spread out on top of me, his head pillowed on my chest, one arm clutching me tight.

I stroke his hair, moving it back from his face before I run my nails through it, scratching lightly. He hums, content, and I can feel his muscles start to relax.

"One of us is going to have to get up to get my bags," I say. "We already ruined one nice piece of clothing tonight, and while I am more than ready to donate a bodysuit to the cause of getting fucked that good, I don't want to lose everything because we're lazy." I run my hand down his back, scratching lightly. "I packed my favorites, after all. I think you'll like some of them too." The way he'd moan on the phone, asking me what I'm wearing, picturing it for himself, leads me to think he'll love seeing those outfits in person. Although if he destroys any more of them, we'll have to go shopping.

That actually sounds nice. Bryce would be a fun shopping companion, because he's ridiculously awed by everything I wear. And maybe we could sneak into a changing room...

"How much did you pack?" he asks, voice muffled against my chest.

I know what he's really asking, though. How long are you staying?

I remove my hand from his hair to stroke down his spine instead. "Two bags worth. All my favorites. Will you come with me back to New York to get the rest? Chase said he'd take me, maybe next week."

His entire body goes still, and then he raises his head slowly so he can look at me. "Mae, are you..." He trails off. Scared to say it, probably.

"I was hoping to stay," I tell him.

"Stay?"

"Like, move in. Give up my apartment. Let Violet stay there; they were practically already running the shop, it made sense. And I rather be here. With you." I swallow, thinking of all the late-night phone calls, dinner and sharing every moment of our day. Telling him things I didn't talk to anyone else about.

And ending the day fingering my own cunt, his voice in my ear, wishing he was actually there.

And now I'm here with him, and it's exactly where I want to be.

"Is that okay?" I check, but I think I already know his answer.

He leans back down and kisses me until I can't breathe, which is answer enough for me.

CHAPTER FORTY

BRYCE

I wake up and I swear it was all a dream.

But her scent permeates everything, every inch of the bed and of me. And I feel her hair against my skin, her warm body against me, her soft breasts still under my head.

She's real. She's here. And she's staying.

And not just for the night. Not just for a fuck. She's staying.

I crack an eye open to check. She's still asleep under me, breathing softly and relaxed. I don't want to look away, but I force myself to look at the pile by the dresser.

Her bags, dragged inside last night when I forced myself out of bed for the bags and a dinner we could eat in bed. They're stacked there, both bags, just waiting for me to make room for her in the closet and dresser.

I'll give her the whole damn thing if she wants it. I'll leave my clothes in a pile on the floor, if it means she'll take up space in this house.

I turn my attention back to her, unable to keep away for even a minute. My mate. My mate, in our bed, satisfied by me, is asleep and looking safe and whole.

I'm more than aware of the coming moon. The wolf in me practically howls, so deeply satisfied to have our mate here with us tonight.

And I was rough with her last night. She didn't seem to mind. That's an understatement. She told me how much she enjoyed herself, multiple times. But if she's sore, and the wolf pushes me to be rough and demanding again tonight...

Can I convince the wolf to be gentle with her, even on the night of the full moon?

Like she can hear that my thoughts are entirely about her, Mae stirs. It's small at first, but then it becomes more obvious she's waking up. I stroke my hand down her arm, wanting her to wake up gently.

The clock on the bedside table tells me it's after ten. A perfect time for my morning-hating mate to wake.

"Good morning, little witch." I kiss her forehead, then both cheeks, then at last her mouth.

Without even opening her eyes, she kisses me back, one hand softly coming up to cup my face, and I lean into it.

"Wouldn't mind waking up this way every morning," she murmurs when she pulls back.

"I can do that." I can do that and so much more. It hits me then, again, that we have a future in front of us now, real and in my grasp. She's here, she's mine, and I can wake her up this way every day forever.

"Want coffee?" I ask, because I don't delude myself that her sleeping until ten will be enough to curb her caffeine addiction. I wonder if there's a pile of stimulant spells shoved in those bags.

She stretches under me. "That sounds good. Can I have your shirt?"

She can have literally anything of mine that she'd like. A shirt is the least of it.

I find my pants from last night and give her a spare shirt, and we make our way downstairs. I fiddle with the coffeemaker and she sits at the counter, and it feels so domestic, so perfect. Like a peek into the future, what every single day forever could be.

It's a damn good image.

***

The image persists for the rest of the day. We move things around to give her half the closet and space in the bathroom. She sets a dozen tiny little bottles of nail polish on the dresser and I can't stop looking at them, smiling every time they catch my eye. It's her mark, a sign she's here, that this is real.

It's not just a change of clothes. It's not temporary. She wouldn't bring them if she didn't intend to be here for a while.

"Do you need anything?" I ask her, looking over the bottle of her shampoo now in the shower. "Anything at all? Want to change the decorations? We can do that."

She laughs. "I think we both know that we're not going anywhere to do any of that today."

Today. The first she's mentioned what today will bring, even obliquely. I pause. "How much do you know about werewolves and the full moon?"

"I know you go a bit feral. More than last night?"

I shrug. I've never spent the full moon with my mate before, and her guess is as good as mine. "I'll be careful with you," I promise, although I have no idea if I can even keep that promise.

"Not too careful, I hope," she says. "I've thought about it a bit, you know."

Oh? From the look in her eyes, I know exactly what type of thinking she's done about it, and I'm half-tempted to roll her into the bed right now to show her what she's been missing out on.

I look at the clock. Moonrise is in three hours.

"Mae?"

"Mhm?"

I grin. "Wear something you won't be too sad if I rip, yeah?"

***

We go outside just before moonrise, joining the mingling crowd of mated wolves, all studiously ignoring each other, making their way to favored spots. True to her word, Mae's wearing the most casual outfit I've ever seen on her, a pair of loose shorts and my own t-shirt. I already want to rip it off her, and the moon hasn't risen yet.

But there's one more thing I have to say to her, while we're both still fully in our right minds to hear it. "Mae, if we go through with this—"

"When we go through with this—"

"I'm going to bite you. I'll bite you and that's it, if you let me bite you then I'm your mate forever."

She steps closer, right up into my space. "Are you saying I'm not already your mate forever?"

I cup her face, turning her jaw so I can look her in the eyes. "You absolutely are."

"Then it's not going to change anything." She puts her hand on my wrist. "You know, Chase, Violet, and I invented all sorts of spells."

I have no idea where this is coming from, but I nod. "I heard."

"Violet thought of this one. We couldn't get it to work without physical contact, so we discarded it, but, well..." I feel something on my wrist, and then it's like my whole body freezes, all my muscles refusing to cooperate.

"Five minute head start," she says, stroking her fingers over what seems like a bracelet on my wrist. She leans in and kisses me, and I can't even kiss her back, causing a growl to build up that I can't release.

"Find me," she whispers, and then she turns to the forest.

CHAPTER FORTY-ONE

MAE

I'm not going to get very far in five minutes. Not when he's known this forest for a thousand years and I'm already lost.

I'm not worried about that. I just want to rile my wolf up a bit.

Running isn't easy. I'm not exactly inclined to run normally, and with what I've hidden under this shirt, my tits are bouncing all over the place, making running damn uncomfortable.

That's okay. I just need to find a spot.

There. A rock, about hip-height. I make my way over, ripping off Bryce's shirt and discarding it onto the ground as I do.

The bra underneath really doesn't deserve to be called a bra in the functional sense. It does absolutely nothing but look good, but that's the entire point.

When I got dressed earlier, I had visions of Bryce ripping it off with his teeth, and the thought makes me shiver.

I can see the moon now, and know my five minutes are up. My wolf will be here any minute.

So I kick off my shorts, leaving just the panties that should hopefully make Bryce crazy, and lean against the rock.

I hear him and turn around to give him a smile as he barrels into the clearing, chest heaving and eyes a little wild.

He still looks like himself. The moon doesn't seem to cause any physical changes. But there's something about his eyes, an intensity there that I've never seen before, a whole new level beyond where he normally is.

It looks like he wants to eat me. Like his every thought is consumed by me, like chasing me down is his whole focus in life.

I shake my ass at him a little, just to tempt the wolf inside him. Just to see what happens.

A shiver passes through me when he growls, and I feel my nipples tighten, rubbing at the barely there material, sending sparks pooling in my belly.

He wants me. He's crazy for me right now, wants me so badly, and with all that focus on me, I feel like I could take on the world.

"Mate," he rasps, voice guttural. "My mate."

"Yours," I agree, because it would be cruel not to, at this point. "Yours, and you're mine, now come here and prove it."

He's on me before I can say anymore, enormous hands cupping my ass, kneading it, making me moan, arching back for him.

When he's had his fill, he spins me around, pressing me back so my thighs are against the rock and he's blocking me in. "You're way too overdressed for tonight," I tell him, tracing the shirt he's still wearing.

The shirt is gone in an instant, and he's already working on his pants before I really process that. I watch him, all hard, flexing muscle, moving faster because I told him to get naked for me.

"How's this going to play out tonight, do you think?" I muse, not really expecting an answer. Chase has already warned me that wolves aren't big on verbal communication under the moon.

Of course, he'd told me they're plenty good at non-verbal communication.

I rest my hips against the rock and spread my thighs, lifting one hand to my breast and kneading. Let that do the talking for me.

He pushes his pants down while entirely focused on what I'm doing, stepping out of them so fast he almost trips himself as he moves towards me, replacing my hand with his own, kneading through the fabric of my bra.

"I thought you'd like this," I tell him, stroking one finger along my other breast, then down my stomach, then feather-light over the panties. "Thought you might like this one. And if it gets damaged—we'll just have to go get more."

Like my words are permission, he uses a claw to slice it down the middle, being very careful to not even nick my skin.

Then he grabs me by the hips and sits me on the rock so he can reach my nipples without bending so far over, wrapping one in his mouth and sucking, making me shove my tits towards him.

He takes the hint, using one hand to massage the other. I moan and arch closer to him.

He growls against my chest, and I think it's a sound of approval.

I get one hand in the hair at the base of his skull, and wrap my legs shakily around him, pulling him closer. "You're good at that," I murmur, more to myself than to him, but he hears it and sucks harder.

I tug lightly at his hair until he gets the point and pulls back. Another growl, but this one in frustration, I think. A man who knows what he wants.

Well, I know what I want too, and I'm not going to be shy about telling him. "I want you inside me," I tell him. I look him over, hard and wanting with hungry eyes, and I think back to how he was last night. My cunt clenches around nothing, desperate to have him inside me again. "I want you to fuck me until I see stars." And then bite me, I don't say, but I don't need to. We both know how tonight ends.

He drags me to the edge of the rock. He's careful about it, like he doesn't want the rough texture of the rock to hurt my skin, which is honestly the last thing I'm worried about right now. Then he falls to his knees with significantly less care.

That's not fucking me until I see stars, but he then tears my panties off with his teeth, just like I fantasized about earlier, and I'm suddenly much more forgiving of this deviation in the plan.

I'm even more forgiving when he buries his head between my thighs, licking my cunt like a desperate man at his last meal, like he's starved for it. He groans against me and I can't help it; I whimper and wrap shaky legs around his head.

That just encourages him further, and he slides two fingers into me all at once, making me throw my head back and moan as he pulls them out and pushes them back in again before crooking them just so.

Gods, I'm going to come. I can feel it building already, spiraling me higher and higher, and I know I can't stop it. "Bryce, I—oh, gods, yes—I'm—I'm going to come, I—" He doesn't stop. If anything, he sets in with even more determination, pushing me over the edge.

I'm sure the entire village can hear me, but then again, I probably won't be the only one to come screaming tonight.

I forcibly relax my thighs, which have tightened on his head, like I intended to hold him to me forever.

He doesn't move, even when I let him go. He just keeps lapping at me with his tongue, and I moan, shivering under his ministrations.

No. I have an agenda. I told him to fuck me, and he's going to fuck me, dammit. Hard and a little feral and so, so good.

I tug on his hair until I have his eyes on me. "Fuck me," I say as firmly as I can. My voice already sounds wrecked, and I spare half a thought for how I'll sound in the morning.

Gods, two days of sex with my werewolf and I'm a mess. A delicious, wet and dripping mess. I can't help but think of what I'll be like in a month. A year.

A decade, a century—I have a lot of life ahead of me. And I'm going to spend it with him. With Bryce, the werewolf still kneeling between my legs and looking up at me like I hung the moon and stars.

"Get inside me, Bryce."

He growls and surges to his feet, grabbing me and lifting me fully off the rock. His hands grab my ass, holding me up and squeezing like he just can't help himself. I wrap my legs around his waist, trying to wiggle to where I want him.

His hold on me is too strong though, and I realize I'm at the wolf's mercy.

I grin and kiss at his neck, then bite lightly at the skin there. He moans loudly, so I nip at his skin again.

So much for me being at his mercy. I can play this game as well as he can. "Fuck me," I tell him, voice muffled by his throat, but I know he can hear me. "Fuck me, Bryce, c'mon—"

He lines me up and sinks me down onto his cock without another word. I gasp, grabbing at his shoulders for purchase, holding on for dear life as he holds perfectly still, bottomed out inside me and letting me get used to the stretch.

I wiggle in his grip, and he growls and just holds me tighter. "Move, dammit," I gasp.

He does.

With just his own strength holding me up, he pounds me hard, moving me on his cock, each stroke deep and firm, making me whine and grab at him tighter.

With his hands busy, I find my own clit, stroking in time with his thrusts, pushing myself closer and closer to the oncoming orgasm.

I tip my head. "Bite me, Bryce." My voice is breathy in a way I don't recognize. "C'mon, mark me, make me yours, my mate—"

It's like the word is a trigger, like it drives him over some sort of edge, because he growls again and repeats the word. "Mate."

Hearing it makes me shiver. Makes me want it even more than I already have these past few days. Mate, and all that entails. Forever.

His teeth sink into my neck.

It hurts, but I'm so close to coming that I've crossed that line where pain is muted and doesn't feel real anymore. Mostly I feel consumed by it, held by him, knowing we're permanently tied together now, and, with one more flick of my clit, I come.

I gasp his name as I do, my free hand digging into his shoulder hard enough to leave indents.

That must send him over the edge, because he pulls his teeth from my neck to roar, enough to shake the trees, enough to split through the forest around us.

He goes to his knees, carefully cradling me so I'm still held to him, hips still moving as much as they can, pumping into me and chasing that high, and I groan and clench around him.

He stops moving a moment later, breathing raggedly. "Mate," he says, voice wrecked, and I smile at him.

"Mate," I agree. I stroke his face, his eyes intent on me, and I hold there for a second. "Let me go?"

He growls but does as I ask, just like I knew he would. I kiss him as a reward for doing so, and then get to my feet and walk away from him.

I can almost feel the weight of his displeasure, but I don't stop. I'm not going far.

I begin to hum and crouch down when I see a telltale rock embedded in the ground. I touch my hand to it, and it begins to glow.

I turn my head to look over my shoulder, smiling at Bryce, who watches me with filthy, undisguised longing. "Good news," I tell him. "I think we'll have an easy enough time renewing that border spell. Say, every full moon?"

If the force of him fucking me the first time I did it made me feel like magic was practically dripping off me, that was a trickle compared to the river of magic in me now. I could light up a city, at this rate.

Bryce, in his current state, doesn't seem to appreciate the finer points of my magic. He prowls closer, a predator stalking his prey. I move from my crouch to my hands and knees, shaking my ass just enough to tell him I'm ready, that I want whatever he's bringing.

Not prey. A trap, luring my wolf in.

He pounces, and I moan, rocking into his hands on my ass, knowing there are hours to go until moonset.

CHAPTER FORTY-TWO

BRYCE

I wake up with my arms full of witch, and I squeeze her closer, breathing her in.

Her scent is different. Still the same underneath it all, still her and perfect, but now there's a layer of me too. My come, yes, but also just me. A part of her, like she's a part of me.

My mate.

I move her hair and crane my head, and sure enough, there's a healing bite on her neck. It's healing cleanly and will disappear in a few hours at most.

But I'll always know it's there. I'll be able to feel it, feel her, and know that we're mates, now and forever.

And when I say forever, I mean it. We have forever.

I've put a lot of thought into our forever since she arrived yesterday. Maybe for longer, if I'm honest. I've been thinking about it since Celia told me to go after her, even if it didn't feel real then. But now that she's here, now that she has my mark, now that this feels real—I have thoughts. And I just need her to wake up so we can plan our lives together.

I'm debating if it's better to keep letting her sleep here in the forest, or if I should carry her back to the house when she stirs.

"Good morning," I say softly, kissing the top of her head while she slowly wakes up.

"Mmm," she groans, but then seems to force herself more awake. "So, you're you again?"

"Was I not me last night?" I ask, genuinely curious. I remember everything that happened, I'm pretty sure. I'm still me, at least I think so. Just a little more driven.

Feral, really, if I'm honest.

"Well, you're usually a better communicator," she says, voice light, and she pushes herself up so she can look at me.

"I thought I communicated just fine last night," I tease when I realize she's smiling.

"Mmm, good enough," she agrees, stretching languorously against me.

"So you liked it?" I have to check.

"I liked it enough that it gave me a giant magical boost. Never mind the border spell; I swear I could've done anything last night."

That's right. That part of the memory had seemed almost unimportant last night, compared to the crystal clear memories of being inside her, but I remember her now, leaving me long enough to do the border spell. "Does it need to be renewed every full moon?"

"With that much power? No way."

"Good," I tell her, stroking her hair back from her face and cupping her jaw. "Because I was thinking we should spend the next full moon somewhere else."

"Oh? Where?"

"That depends on you," I say. "There's an atlas at the house. We'll open it, you'll point to somewhere. And we'll go. And when you're done there, you'll point somewhere else, and we'll go there too."

She laughs a little, defensive and disbelieving. "You can't just go."

"I can. I will. I was going to," I assure her. "My trip to New York for next week? I was going to beg you to let me stay with you. Celia and I talked." I swallow. "I'm not giving up all my responsibilities to this pack. I like what I do. But Celia is right. Other people can do some of it. And I have a beautiful, wonderful mate now. I need to show her the world. Only I can do that. Let someone else convince the humans to cut down someone else's forest. They'll figure it out."

"You were going to stay in New York? You don't like New York."

"I like being where you are. I'd prefer it was here, or any place you want to go. Not that shop that made you miserable and clogged my damn nose." I wrinkle my nose at the memory, at not being able to smell her when she was right there. She laughs disbelievingly.

"I still have to go back to that shop, you know. I own a third of it and Violet can't work all the spells without me."

"And I still want to do some work for this pack. We'll figure it out. Make it work."

She stops for a moment, going stock-still, and I can see her brain whirring behind her eyes. I hold still too, waiting for whatever conclusion she'll come to. "You'll really leave?"

I can't resist it anymore. I lean up, cradling her face to draw her to me, kissing her hard enough that she hopefully can read how much I'm willing to do this with her. Eager to do this with her.

"I've seen the world and haven't given a fuck about it," I tell her, an inch from her lips. "I did my job and I went home. Now, let me see it all over again with you. Let me appreciate the experience this time."

She kisses me again, and I swear I feel a spark between us, sealing the deal.

***

This is the second time we've left the forest half dressed, with Mae wearing my shirt. But I hadn't left any traces of the scraps of underwear she wore to tease me, and her shirt and shorts disappeared wherever she tossed them.

I could probably sniff them out, because I could track her scent across the entire village. But I don't mention that to her, just helping her into my shirt.

Unlike last time, no one is looking at us. We're certainly not the only couple making their way home after a wild night.

196

"I am sorry about your clothes," I tell her, remembering what I'd done to them. Maybe not sorry enough to truly regret it, especially now that she's wearing absolutely nothing but my shirt. But sorry because I know she likes her clothes.

"You think I didn't know what would happen to them? That was the plan, Bryce. Now you need to take me shopping."

That idea interests me. A lot. Watching her try on options. Maybe model them for me...

"As soon as you want," I manage to say, mind already thinking of where the best shopping in the world might be. Where can I take her?

We get to our house before I can decide, and I go to start the coffee as soon as we shut the door behind us, knowing what my mate wants.

My mate, forever. She's here. She's with me, she's here and she's mine and I'm hers and we are starting our forever, exactly how we should.

Most mated wolves don't show their faces the day after the full moon, preferring to take it easy. Catch up on sleep, cuddle a bit, hold each other close. Settle back into everyday life after the feral fuck the night before.

I've never experienced it before today, but I remember easily the misery I'd incur if I interrupted Celia and Bethany's post-moon days with anything less than the direst of emergencies. Knowing that, I don't plan to leave the house, never mind let Mae out of my sight.

I bring her coffee and an atlas, sinking onto the couch with her and pulling her into my side. She curls in close, opening the book on our laps and drinking her coffee while she begins to peruse it.

***

Bethany invites the entire family to breakfast the next morning. Invites may be too mild a word, because Bethany has perfected sweet statements that are actually orders.

But when it's breakfast that she's offering, no one argues.

The table at her and Celia's house is laden with food, enough to feed an army. Or enough to feed five wolves, a demon, and a witch.

Chase grins at Mae, a slow, wicked thing. "So, you survived."

She actually swats the back of his head, making him laugh. "Yes, I survived, you asshole."

"The light show gave it away a bit," Heath murmurs.

I growl. "Focus on your own damn business next time." How in the world do they have time to worry about us during the full moon?

Heath raises an eyebrow, not backing down from my growling. "You lit up the forest, Bryce. Again. No one could miss that."

Callum clears his throat and we stop. Right. He probably did miss it. He's been waiting for his mate nearly as long as I have, and I doubt he was running around the forest last night. I doubt he was even outside, not wanting to run into any happy couples.

I feel a pang of sympathy for my brother, and I hope he finds them soon.

Chase doesn't drop the subject, though. I think he just enjoys needling Mae, wanting to get a reaction out of her. "Okay, but you should know that the whole village is in a bit of a tizzy."

"Because of a little light?" Mae asks, clearly skeptical.

"No, because they're thinking there's finally going to be a Crae heir. You know, what with all the fucking you two did last night."

My mouth falls open, and I gape like a fish. I haven't even thought about that. Hadn't known other people were thinking about it either, although Chase is probably telling the truth. He always has his finger on the pulse of what's going on.

Does Mae want that? What if we did, last night...

Mae tosses her head. "Yeah, well. They can wait. I know you're all ancient, but haven't you all heard of birth control?"

Something inside me eases. Birth control. Okay. We're fine.

Celia sits down at the table, reaching for Bethany, who is still puttering around with food and dragging her closer, pulling her into her lap. "Are you saying never, Mae? Because it's not the end of the world—there's four of us, we're not in a leadership crisis here—but it would take some planning."

"You can't ask her that right now," I protest. My mate decided to be my mate two days ago. She's known me for a matter of months. She's sixty.

Mae doesn't need me to defend her, though. "I'm saying that I have a lot to do and a kid would cramp my style," she says. "I'm saying that I have a werewolf to fuck in exotic locations, and I think pregnancy would be a drag on that. Ask me in a century."

Everyone goes absolutely silent, but Chase grins. "Alright then."

Bethany sighs. "One normal breakfast."

Celia squeezes her gently. "That's too much to ask and you know it."

Mae gives me a look as if challenging me, as if daring me to question her decision. But I just reach for her hand and squeeze it, more than glad to think of all the places we'll go, the things we'll do. One thing at a time. We have a life to live before we think of the Crae heir.

Speaking of our life to live, it's about time I tell them what we've decided. "We're leaving in two days."

"New York?" Callum asks.

"No."

"We have a list," Mae says, and she keeps her voice even, but I can see the excitement in her eyes.

"Of exotic locations to fuck in?"

Mae is saved from having to answer by her cell phone ringing. She pulls it out of a sinfully tight pocket that I have no idea how it fits inside in the first place and picks up. "Hello? Violet—Violet, slow down."

She pulls the phone away from her ear, which does nothing to mute the panicked babbling we can all hear.

I hear one word, repeated and clear above all the others.

Clay.

CHAPTER FORTY-THREE

MAE

Clay is there. Clay is there, inside the store, where Violet is.

He's not standing outside. He got in.

"We have to go," I say urgently to the room at large. "We have to—Clay will—Violet—"

Bryce takes my hand and draws me to him, squeezing. "We'll go," he promises. "Chase, I'll pay whatever toll you need to take. Just get us there."

"Me too," Heath, Celia, Bethany, and Callum say about the same time.

Chase frowns. "That's a big transport, can't do that many at once—and you wouldn't want me to, the energy penalty would knock you on your ass for a week."

Heath puts his hand on Chase's arm. "I'll pay it," he says. "Two trips. But we have to go now."

Chase nods, grabs for Bryce, and then we disappear, reappearing an instant later in the shop.

Violet is nowhere to be seen. Upstairs, hopefully, locked in the apartment, although I doubt that a simple, totally non magical door lock would keep Clay out for long.

But Clay isn't chasing them down. He's standing at a display, hands held behind his back, examining the contents.

"Get the fuck out of my store," I snarl. Heath and Chase disappear again, but I don't care. The lack of backup doesn't bother me.

Clay is my problem. My cousin. Greta left him to me and now I'll solve this.

And I feel Bryce step up behind me, big and imposing over my shoulder, ready to kill Clay if he needs to.

Gods, I hope it doesn't come to that. I don't want to explain that to his mother.

"Cousin," Clay greets, like we met casually on the street. "Thanks for changing the ownership papers. It finally broke Greta's damn boundary wards."

Boundary wards. My brain spins, trying to fit all the pieces together. But that's it, isn't it? Why he never just walked in. Why every time he came in, he specifically asked for permission first.

My permission. Because it was my shop.

But it's not just my shop anymore. It's ours now, the three of us, and whatever protections against Clay Greta put in place broke.

I scan the room. It looks mostly okay, with a sprung rope trap by the door Clay obviously evaded. Still, not much damage was done. Violet got out before Clay resorted to blatant violence.

"Get out."

"I wasn't sure you were coming back," Clay says. "I thought you might have just given up."

"Well, I'm here. And I'm saying get the fuck out of my shop."

He turns around finally. There's an ugly gash on his face, no doubt from one of our traps. His eyes look past the point of being rational. Like something's chasing him, maybe. "Why do you care, Mae? You never wanted it and I need it."

I take a step forward. "Why do you care so much, Clay?" I take another step. "You never needed this place. You could do so much without it."

His face is drawn, and his hands shake as he raises them as if to physically shove me away. "Don't come any closer."

I don't listen, taking another step. "Why?"

"I made promises. The type you don't break."

"Stupid of you," Bryce growls from behind me.

Clay's eyes flick momentarily to the werewolf hovering behind me, like he's finally realized the biggest threat in the room. "Wouldn't expect you to understand," he sneers.

I take the moment where his attention is off me to step forward again. And then I hear two pops.

I scream when the pain rips through my arm. I can't help it; it feels like a hot knife dragging through my skin, like someone is twisting it at the same time they push me away.

I land on my back and hands are there immediately, but they're not Bryce's hands, because Bryce is already charging at Clay, head down, nails already shifting to claws.

"You're okay," Celia tells me, her voice somehow calm despite everything. Her brother roars, and I watch in horror as blood seeps from his own arm, under his shirt, but he doesn't go to the ground. He does, however, have to fight to keep his feet. Celia winces, but doesn't change her tone. "It'll heal fast."

"You stupid werewolf," Clay snaps, stepping back. "Stay out of things you don't know."

Bryce roars as whatever spell Clay has placed attacks him again, impeding his progress, but then he reaches my cousin and rakes a clawed hand down his chest.

Gods, he's going to kill him. He's going to kill Clay in this shop.

I take a shaky breath. "Under the counter, there's a half dozen vials, I need them right now," I bite out, and I hear footsteps moving to get them for me. Something inside me warms at them listening, no questions asked, but I'm too focused on Bryce pummeling my cousin and bleeding freely all the while to really think about it.

The vials are shoved into my hands, and I uncap one, looking up to aim my throw.

But Bryce is still there, in the way, and there's no way to throw this without hitting him.

"Bryce! Get out of there and come here!" My voice is hoarse, and I just have to hope he'll listen if he can even hear me.

His eyes snap to mine immediately, and it takes him less than a second to listen. He turns his back on Clay and moves to me, going to his knees next to me, reaching for me.

Which is all very sweet, but I still have a cousin who's proven he's not averse to doing serious bodily harm and scaring the shit out of my business partner to take this place. I use all the strength I have and hurl the bottle at Clay.

And it's like a fire bursts from contact, burning hot and bright and quick. And when the fire burns down, Clay is on the ground, dazed and completely motionless.

I pick up another bottle, just in case. But the first one seems to have done the job.

"Help me up," I say to Bryce.

He hesitates. "You're injured."

I look at his arm and chest, cut a dozen or more times. "You're one to talk. Help me up."

He does, and I walk carefully over to where Clay sprung his trap.

There's nothing obvious in the area, so the spell must be on Clay himself. This isn't my type of magic. I feel the slash on my arm and the pain that it brought. This is dark magic, the type Greta always worried about from Clay.

And I know, deep down, that this is the least of what he can do.

Not knowing the spell, I have to make some guesses about how to approach him safely. I move forward before Bryce can stop me, and grit my teeth while getting cut on the arm twice before I can unclasp the necklace from his neck. It's too ugly to be anything my cousin ever would have bought for himself.

Bryce grabs me, and I fling the necklace into the corner no one is standing in. I brace myself to be wrong, but no further cuts come.

Chase looks at the corner interestedly. "Ryder might like that," he says. Then, heedless of what might happen, he scoops it up and disappears again.

I walk right up to my cousin, still lying dazed on the ground. "You'll leave," I tell him, as fiercely as I can. "You'll get lost. Get out of New York. I'll re-do the warding and you'll never even think about this shop again. Get lost. And if you don't, then I'll let him at you again," I threaten, jerking a finger to Bryce. "Realize that the only reason I didn't let him finish it is because I don't want to return you to your mother in a body bag. But I will if you threaten us again."

He's frozen as a statue, but I don't think I imagine the hate in his eyes, burning white hot and ready to do serious damage to me and mine. Whatever meager protection being family had bought me, I know it's gone forever now. So I need to act before he can. "Someone help me toss him out?" I ask.

Callum steps closer. "My absolute pleasure," he says, already grabbing Clay by his shoulders to haul him up, not exactly worrying about being gentle.

I watch him drag my cousin—my cousin, who I don't recognize anymore, who I can't imagine as the young man who Greta and I spent so much time with—out of the shop, and I sink back into Bryce's waiting arms. We did it. It's done.

***

There's a perfectly normal human first aid kit under the counter, meant for the occasional magical misfire. Bryce insists he'll be fine, but if he's going to insist on looking at my arm, then I'm going to insist on looking at all his cuts, too. Chase reappears after a few minutes, and Heath grumbles at him while bandaging his arm. So we patch each other up at the counter, and when Violet is brought back downstairs by Bethany, they insist on giving each of us a healing crystal.

Once again, I'm nearly positive the crystal isn't enchanted in any way, but I don't argue.

Callum comes back in, closing the door firmly behind him. "Left him in a dumpster," he informs me.

I should feel something, I suppose. I can't make myself.

"I'm going to re-lay the ward," I tell Violet. "I've been thinking about it, and I think it's just a more concentrated version of what I did for the village. I can do it." But here comes the awkward part. I clear my throat. "So, if everyone would get lost for an hour or so."

No one moves. I clear my throat again.

"Seriously?" Chase asks.

"What do you want from me? I've learned how to power the spell and I'm not going to fuck around with testing new methods right now."

"You're *not* going to fuck around?" he mutters.

Bryce holds me close, pulling me into his still-bare chest. "You heard my mate. Get lost."

They all file out the door, one after the other. As soon as we're alone, Bryce goes over to lock the door and then picks me up, carrying me into the backroom. "An hour isn't as much time as I'd want, little witch," he rumbles in my ear. "But I think I can make you come hard enough that you'll be able to power your spell."

***

When the spell is done, and our clothes back on, and we're just waiting for the others to come back, Bryce holds me, his big arms wrapped gently around me. He's got bandages across his arms and on his chest, but he keeps insisting on pressing right up against me, like they don't hurt in the slightest. "Do we need to stay in New York for a while?"

We. Because there will be no more of this messing around. Where one goes, so does the other. End of story.

"No. Violet can handle this. And Clay can't come back. We're leaving." I sigh, leaning back against him. "We're going to do everything we said we would."

He kisses my temple. "Can't wait to start our life together," he promises, and I close my eyes, letting myself think of the beautiful life to come.

CHAPTER FORTY-FOUR

MAE

Three Months Later

"Are you going to stay out here all night?"

I turn away from the light show that is the sky to find my mate, leaning against the sliding door frame of the cabin we've rented.

"I'm staying as long as that keeps going," I say, pointing up.

He sighs, but comes outside, sliding onto the oversize outdoor couch with me, pulling me into his arms. "We can see the northern lights at home sometimes, you know," he says.

"Well, I haven't yet, so I'm watching them here." I purposefully wiggle to get a bit more comfortable, moving me essentially into his lap. He just holds me tighter.

It's quiet for a minute when we watch the sky. His hand is stroking up and down my side, although through my thick sweater, I'm not really feeling it.

"Rental's up in two days," he says, voice a breath against my ear. "Where to next?"

"Somewhere warm," I say. The cozy cabin has been charming, but I could do with some sun. Enchanted clothes or not, the tip of my nose has almost frozen off here.

"Done."

"With a beach."

"Done," he says. "Do you need to go shopping for a bathing suit?"

I move against his lap. He's definitely interested in that idea. "You know what? Excellent idea. Let's do that first."

And the full moon's coming up soon, too. Maybe a private beach, just for the night. Where we can be just us, and see if fucking on the sand is as good as the forest...

After all, if we have forever, I'm eager to explore all options.

CHAPTER FORTY-FIVE

BRYCE

CURRENT DAY

When Celia dismisses us after her declaration that we're essentially going to war, Mae and I make our way back to our house.

"How can I help?" she asks, leaning against the kitchen counter. "I can work on some spells, especially if I can collaborate with Marielle and Chase. But I'm not a soldier, Bryce. I don't know how to be, not yet."

"You don't have to be a soldier," I say. I'm barely a soldier, although I've been to war, killed my share. And I probably will again, before this is over.

But first and foremost, I'm a diplomat. "We've met people on our travels," I tell her. Most of them are irrelevant to our current situation, but they aren't all irrelevant. "A lot of them I'd consider potential allies. I'm going back to them to start making actual alliances. To tell them what's out there. Are you coming?"

The smile she gives me is a little wicked and warms something inside me. "I go where you go," she says. "Let's make a list. I'm putting New York at the top."

I swallow. "Why New York?" I ask. We go back every few months or so, for Mae to help Violet with some spells and check on the shop. We never stay there long.

"Because there are some witches I want to talk to," she says. "And I want to get them on our side. And I might be the only one they'll listen to."

Witches... I shiver thinking about it, but she's right. If they'll listen to anyone, unite for anyone, it'll be Mae.

"No time to waste, then," I say.

She tilts her head, a look I've long learned by now, already stepping closer, helplessly drawn to her. "Maybe a few minutes to waste," she murmurs, fingertips tilting my head so she can lean up for a kiss.

Maybe a few minutes. And then we have allies to win.

CHAPTER FORTY-SIX

CLAY

The minute I failed to deliver on my promises, all I've been given is shit work.

Sometimes literally. Almost always bloody, and not always other people's blood.

The shop. That damned shop, Greta's pride and joy, with magic baked into the walls and a steady following of magic users ready to buy whatever the proprietor is selling. I thought it'd be so easy. Something to offer, and so easy to get. So easy to give.

If I thought I had any real use to this group before everything fell apart, the day Mae kicked me out of that damn shop for good fully corrected that opinion. I made a promise, and I failed to deliver.

And now I'm paying the price.

I walk faster through the city, turning down the block. But the footsteps keep following me. And they're gaining.

I can't go any faster with my limp. I'm practically defenseless when it comes to spells right now. They've been sure to use every drop of power I have to give at any given time.

A bolt of cold hits me in the back, knocking the air out of my lungs. I fall to my knees, gasping.

"What do you want?" I demand when I can get my breath.

Careful, light footsteps move around me. And unlike a moment ago, they seem in no hurry.

They stop in front of me, and my eyes trail up the legs, the body, to find a face with pointed ears and icy eyes.

"There you are," she says, stepping closer, voice dripping with ice and contempt. "I have a job for you, witch."

LOOKING FOR MORE?

Receive a special bonus scene about Bryce and Mae if you sign up for my newsletter at www.addyjameswriter.com! Subscribers receive exclusive bonuses and are always the first to know updates about upcoming projects.

WHAT TO READ NEXT?

Want to meet more of the Craes? Heath is next—watch him meet his mate in the middle of a war, and the two of them plot to overthrow a regime while falling in love.

***

The mist goes on for so long that it takes me a minute to process the change in smell. I've arrived on the other side, then, but Demonheim is exactly as tricky and unnavigable as Ryder and Hannah both warned.

The fog is even thicker here, like the realm itself is trying to stymie my progress. Fucking demon magic, inscrutable and complicated and fucking irritating.

All magic is irritating, but demon magic is a special brand, relying on complicated deals and clauses, always unapproachable to outsiders, which is clearly evident by the very realm fighting to keep me out.

I suppose it's a defense mechanism. Demonheim is, after all, designed as a sort of prison, a place to keep the very worst of us, the ones we choose not to kill for whatever reason. Demons are gods-designed to be the jailors, and it makes sense for a jail to be unnavigable by everyone but the jailors.

The gods think of everything, I suppose. Except for the fact that I am a wolf, and they can design this land however they want. My senses won't lie to me.

So I close my eyes and ignore all the extraneous stimuli, taking a deep breath.

My eyes shoot open.

I didn't expect to scent anything in particular; I just wanted to determine a way forward. But the minute I open my wolf senses fully, I find the sweetest, most alluring scent I've ever smelled in my life.

Like the spiced apple cider Bethany makes in the autumn, only a thousand times more potent. I've never scented anything like it before, but the wolf in me knows what I'm scenting before my mind can even process it.

Mate.

I close my eyes again, taking off through the mist at a run.

***

The scent grows sharper, so I assume I'm getting closer. *My mate, my mate, my mate.* The thought consumes me entirely. I can't think of Hannah, or Ryder, or the struggle for the sovereignty of Demonheim. All I know is what's in front of me, where I must go.

Mate.

I've waited nearly six centuries for my mate. If they're here, now, if the waiting is finally over—

The air changes, and I dare to open my eyes to see where I am in this labyrinthian realm. The mist has weakened, revealing to me a scene that makes my heart thump loud enough I'm surprised I'm not immediately noticed.

I'm in a hallway, dark stone seemingly entombing me here, the narrow hall-way forcing travel in one direction. But that's okay, because standing at the end is the most beautiful man I've ever seen.

This must be my mate. This man, this beautiful man—sandy hair, obsidian demon horns poking out of his loose curls, and eyes so wide and deep when he sees me. He's my mate, and I can feel it in my bones, like something snapping into place. Like the whole world is sharper, brighter, now that he's here in front of me.

I stop moving, my muscles refusing to work. I want nothing more than to go to him, to wrap him in my arms, to fall to my knees in front of him, but he's completely still with his surprise, and I don't want to startle him further.

His eyes trail over me, moving too fast. "You're Hannah's contact?" He looks around surreptitiously, like he's waiting for enemies to jump out from the shadows. For all I know, that could be an actual concern here.

I want to tell him yes. I want to tell him what I'm doing here, that I've come to help. But what comes out is only, "You're my mate."

It's not surprising, perhaps, considering the wolf in me. We're always going to think about our mates before anyone or anything else; we can't be blamed for our single-minded devotion. But it doesn't seem to soothe my mate.

His frantic staring grows somehow more desperate. "Here?" he rasps. I'm not sure exactly what he's reacting to, so I just watch. "Now?"

"Here," I agree. "Now." I step forward, drawn to him. "I'm Heath."

"Chase," he says, stepping closer as if he too can't resist. "Can I—"

I don't know what he's asking for, so I wait for him to elaborate. "Demons don't know our mates on sight," he mutters, and I don't bother to correct that sight has nothing to do with it. For a wolf, everything is about scent. His smell is divine and I desperately ache for more of it.

"We need touch," he continues. "So, can I..."

I nod eagerly, walking over to him. I must look like a desperate child, but I couldn't care less. This is my mate. If he wants to touch me, then I would walk through fire to let him.

His hand lands on mine, a gentle, tentative touch. The touch is barely there, scarcely a brush. And I'm not some green young thing, so a single touch should not make me feel better than anything in the past ever has. And yet it's a shock to my body, an overwhelming feeling like my heart has stopped and restarted just for this one man.

Chase's eyes are closed in what looks like rapture. "Chase?" I murmur, turning my hand under his so I can stoke his fingers.

He shudders like I grabbed his cock. "Gods, that is something," he murmurs.

"What is it?" I ask, because touching my mate feels like a divine revelation, but Chase is very clearly feeling something physical right now.

"Mates, the energy..." he shakes his head. "You wouldn't understand, but it's a purer form of energy. Purer than any other demon bargain. And I've heard about it, but..." He shakes his head again. "I get it now."

He's right, I don't understand, but I'm irrationally pleased that I'm already able to make my mate feel good, and I haven't even shown him what I can do with my tongue yet.

I lean in closer and take a long draw of Chase's scent, letting it fill every inch of me.

I owe my sister an apology for every time I criticized her for being distracted by her mate. This is like an impossible loop, his scent drawing me in further and further, blinding me to everything else.

But then a nagging thought forces its way in, reminding me of where we are. This is not the place to fall into my mate like this. I step back, forcing myself to focus so I can survey my surroundings.

This hallway is too exposed, and simultaneously too enclosed. Anyone could come upon us, and we'd have no chance of escape.

Chase, seemingly, has the same thought. "Some of the king's advisors are right through that door," he mutters. "So unless you want to start this fight now, we need to move."

"Do you have somewhere we can go?" I ask. I'm slightly ashamed to admit that only half my mind is on planning for war.

"Yes. We'll be—well, it's as safe as anywhere else is around here."

And that's all I can ask for, really. So I nod, taking his hand again, some instinct driving me, as if he's going to walk away and leave me here. And I can't have that.

And if I get to see the slack-jawed look on his face when our skin touches again? Then that's just another incentive to not stop touching him.

"I don't know how to get anywhere else," I manage to explain, tearing my eyes from his face to make myself think more clearly. "So you have to lead the way."

I can feel him staring at me, can smell his scent shifting, growing somehow even sweeter. "Chase?" I prompt, voice a little breathier than I'd like.

He forcibly turns away from me, although I note with pride that he doesn't drop my hand. "Alright," he rasps, and then turns his attention rather resolutely to the wall to our left.

Only it's not a wall anymore. It's a corridor, and I do my best not to gape at it. "If I fucking knew how to do that..." I mutter.

Chase doesn't acknowledge that, just grips my hand tighter and pulls me down the corridor.

ALSO BY ADDISON JAMES

Crae Romance

Callum

Bryce

Heath

Celia

Silas

Estrid

Supernatural Christmas

A Werewolf for Christmas

A Recipe for Love

Standalones

The Heat Cure

Dragon's Treasure

ABOUT THE AUTHOR

Addison James is a romance book author from New England. They are obsessed with all things mythical, mystical, and magical. A lifelong fantasy reader, that evolved to fantasy romance as they grew up. Addison always has a story to tell and is excited to introduce you to their world of fantasy romance. Addison can be reached through Tiktok, Instagram, or Threads (@Addyjameswriter), through email at addyjames@addyjameswriter.com, or through their website, www.addy jameswriter.com.